Dirt

By Teffanie Thompson

BROWN GIRLS BOOKS

Houston,Texas*Washington,D.C.*Raleigh/Durham,NC

Brown Girls Books, LLC
www.browngirlsbooks.com

ISBN:
9781944359225 (digital)
9781944359331 (print)

First Brown Girls Books, LLC trade printing
Manufactured and Printed in the United States of America

Acknowledgments

Thank you, Square, my great-great grandfather.

Thank you, Imhotep, my great-great son. Thank you for reading and rereading and rereading the latest newest version of the many edits of this project.

Thank you, Rose Thompson and George Thompson, my parents, for their love and support.

I would like to thank Dianne Hess for planting the seeds of contemporary historical middle grade fiction in my mind garden.

Thank you. Loving appreciation goes to Dr. Tonea Stewart for sharing her family's story with the world in which *Dirt*'s scene, the burning of Square Thompson's eyes, was based in part, on the character account inspired by Tonea Stewart.

Thank you, Seton. My Seton Family Rocks! I would like to thank Karen Williams for requiring me to expand Dirt from a picture book to a novel.

Thank you–Danielle, Lisa, Susan, Ellen! Thank you for being the best and most loving critique partners eva.

Thank you Leslie Davis Guccione for your belief and your DMisms.

Thank you,Heidi.

Thank you, story coach, Adrea. Thank you, author coach, Anjanette.

Thank you, Travis White for traveling with me to Henderson, Texas to visit the land.

Thank you, Brown Girls Publishing – ReShonda Tate Billingsley, Malachi Bailey (Brown Boy), and Jacquelin Thomas.

Thank you. I would like to thank my beautiful great-great daughters, Abby and Halima.

Thank you. Thank you to my great-great-great husband, Farmer Guy/Matt Hanson, for providing a container in which *Dirt* could finally manifest.

You are love.

To my Brother: Anthony 'Wali/Zin' Mills
1973-2016

"Always give obedience and respect to your Mother and Father, for obedience and respect will come to be two major keys of survival; which will bring about an infinite love and respect from others..."

Shem Em Hotep - Uncle Ant(10/13/1996)

Dirt

Dirt cradles the seed.
She carves paths to destiny,
And houses our roots.

Teffanie Thompson

Chapter 1

I walked in from school and Mom immediately turned off her DVR'd *How to Get Away with Murder*. This was major. Mom never turned off Shonda. My stomach felt funny because I had a feeling that this had something to do with me.

"Ms.Peake phoned today," she said.

Mom faked a calm voice and rose from the chocolate leather sofa. Her hips pushed a stack of mail from the credenza and sent it fluttering to the floor. A shiny family reunion reminder postcard winked up at me. She stopped dangerously close to me. Except for the Old Navy flip-flops and the scowl, Mom looked exactly like she did when I left this morning. Her flawless Halle Berry haircut didn't move an inch, but her animal print maroon, orange, and yellow long African dress swayed with each of her movements.

"Hello, beautiful mother. Did she find my phone?" I asked. I was hoping the hopeful tone of my voice would soften whatever she seemed worked up about.

"No, something more serious. You lost your phone again? We can talk about that later," Mom replied.

What had I done wrong? I passed my finals. I paid my fines. This year I actually found all of my textbooks to turn in before the last day of school. No trouble this week. I didn't leave wet towels on the floor in the bathroom. I don't think. Wait, Ms. Peake wouldn't call about wet towels. I didn't know what I had done. These days anything could upset Mom.

"Actually, your teacher informed me that once again you barely passed reading."

I looked up and rolled my head back to rest on top of my backpack to prepare for the speech. The brown and white mural on our front entry ceiling pulled at my vision—colored like root beer floats.

Art fanatics visited our house just to see our ceiling. John Biggers composed one of his last murals, a replica of "Family Unity," in our house.

I think Mom asked Mr. Biggers to paint his masterpiece in the entryway so random strangers wouldn't ramble too far into our house to see his work.

Right now, I wished I could sit backward in the spiral tree trunks with the kids in the painting. The magical colors of the mural blended night with day, and earth with sky. Four kids sat motionless while red dirt from the ground danced with the night stars and sun rays surrounding them.

Next, Mom would tell me about how much money she and Dad paid for the Alain Locke Academy. She'd remind me how many Black people died so that I could live free and read. Why couldn't I live free, and not read?

"Look at me when I'm talking to you."

I nodded from the kids in the trance back to her.

She inched closer to me, and then stopped. She couldn't get any closer.

"Washington, I taught you how to read and I know that you read well. So, if at twelve years old, you don't want to take school seriously, we won't take anything seriously. I've cancelled your enrollment in summer league basketball."

Mom had my full attention now. I slapped my hands over my face to stop the stinging under my eyelids. "No basketball?"

I dropped my arms to my sides. That escalat-ed super fast. Cancelled? My team would never understand. My coach would never understand. I couldn't let them down. This summer we planned to go all the way—Nationals in Las Vegas.

"Don't cry now. You can't just be able to shoot a ball through a net and wind up playing professional basketball. You have to go to college. And in college, you have to do what? Read. Michael Jordan, Kobe Bryant, and LeBron James all went to college. Why are you looking at me like that?" She took in a deep breath and let out an irritated sigh.

I rocked back and forth on my heels. Should I answer? "Mom, two of them didn't even go to college. And I'm not crying." Everyone knew that Kobe and LeBron went into the NBA straight out of high school. Everyone except Mom.

Her glare signaled I shouldn't have corrected her. The calm voice vanished. "You know what? All those Globetrotters did, *I think*? That's not the doggoned point, Washington." She balled her fists on her hips. "The point is your teacher feels you need summer reinforcement and wants to enroll you in summer academy. I love you, Washington, and I know how much you enjoy basketball, but I have to say that I agree with her. This year you are going to summer school..."

Mom kept talking, but I could only hear four words repeating in my head. Summer school...nobasketball. Summer school...no basketball. Summer school... no basketball?

No basketball.

Chapter 2

❧

I couldn't listen to the speech anymore. A wave of relief swept over me when Mom strolled over to the couch, sat down, and clicked the remote. Mom was back in hashtag *H-T-G-A-W-M* mode. I rushed toward the steep stairs, taking them one at a time to the second level.

A real picture, which looked fake, of President Barack Obama and Mom began the line-up of photos on the stair wall. A photograph of my father's father, George Square Thompson hung next to Mom's photo. Grandpa George sat in a blue armchair with his legs crossed at the knee. He wore a stiff, white buttoned down shirt and starched boot cut jeans with real Western boots underneath. He was pressed and perfect from head to toe.

He'd been missing for eight years. The last time anyone ever saw him was at one of our family reunions. Everyone who knew him said that I acted a lot like him. I wished I could have met him again to know if that were true.

Next came the photos of ancient people in fancy frames. They were Black; their pictures were black and white. Light flickered over framed glasses and made the smiling people laugh.

I never made it upstairs without at least glancing at a particular portrait of the man in the centered frame. Sometimes I gave him a head nod or a fist bump. Sometimes I even spoke to him.

I mirrored him. He mirrored me.

We had the same golden brown oval shaped face, the same forehead above the same two thin, perfectly arched, black eyebrows. Our same wide Thompson noses stuck out at the spot under the space between our eyes. I guessed he didn't want to cut his hair either. He pulled his shiny, black hair into a ponytail. I sported an Afro. Square, my great, great, great grandfather tightened his lips into a straight line. He didn't laugh.

"What's up, Square?" I mouthed.

I finished climbing the stairs and stomped into my room.

Why did college have to mean everything to my parents? Layered pennants from Black universities wallpapered three of my four bedroom walls. They covered the fourth wall, the purple and gold one, with streamers and newspaper clippings from

Prairie View A & M, both of my parents' first college. They met there.

I slid off my backpack, and let it plunk to the floor next to my state-of-the-art gaming center. I glanced at the glowing basketball rim above my closet door, a lit neon hoop without a net. Dad mounted it, but Mom said the net looked tacky. The only decoration in the entire room posted for me. My lucky hoop, I could score from any angle in my room.

No ball. I scanned my bed. Where was it? Again and again I'd asked Mom to leave my ball on my bed. I hated having to search for it. Last Friday, she moved it all the way downstairs and to the garage. I couldn't go back down there yet. Not today.

From the middle of the room, standing on the circular Prairie View rug, I dove onto my bed. Ooww, I could have broken my neck. Who put a basketball under a stack of pillows? Really?

I grabbed the ball and practiced finger spinning. What a sucky last day of sixth grade this had been.

I lost my phone, and after an entire school year, I finally asked Imani to be my girlfriend. I loved that she played on the boys' 'A' team, the only girl. Imani even shoots threes. I could never tell what she would do or say, even during a game.

She had a game face, a pretty game face. When I asked, she just said, "You know I can't do that," then turned and walked away.

Now this. I just don't get grown-ups. They're crazy. Basketball, the one thing that got me to do anything right and Mom takes that from me. I thought the rule was no pass, no play. Not… you passed, you couldn't play. If that were really the rule, Mom's art gallery would be closed by now. She surely wasn't passing there. She was barely even working there.

Basketball greats mastered spinning of a basketball on their fingertips. The ball got going; the whirling black lines disappeared into the dark orange.

Some players, the crazy ones, did anything to save a traveling ball that's about to go out- side the lines. On my team, we called that teammate flying out of bounds, a F.O.O.B, kind of like a fool. Boys leapt out of bounds, slammed into a brick wall, and still saved the ball. That's a F. O. O. B. or M.V.F, the Most Valuable F.O.O.B. Sometimes the F.O.O.B. was me.

After practice once, a group of older boys began bugging Imani next to the James Meredith Gym about how she needed to play with girls instead of men. There were three of them following behind her.

I flew out of bounds. I thrust my basketball with all my strength and hit the tallest in the head.

All three spun toward me. One of them recognized me from a basketball tournament as 'the boy who couldn't miss a three,' Mini - Curry. They asked me about what high school I would attend and my favorite NBA players. They seemed to forget about Imani and the slam to the head. I'm glad they did.

Before I threw that ball, I didn't know what would happen next, and I didn't care. That's what flying out of bounds was—when you just didn't care. I felt like that now. I should just run away.

"Washington, come down. Your dad's home," Mom called up the stairs.

I liked Dad's lectures better than Mom's, except for the trivia near the end. Maybe he'd take my side this time. With my ball in hand, I raced downstairs.

Dad was seated in his chair with a crisp *Houston Informer* folded on his lap. "Hey, Dad, what's up?"

"I think you know what's up," he responded. "Your mother tells me that you barely pulled up that reading grade. You struggled in that class all year. What's the problem?" Dad's quiet voice normally made me feel safe, but the way he twisted the newspaper as he spoke caused me to cringe.

"Ms. Peake makes us read out loud," I answered. "And I hate it. I ask her if I can do something else, anything else."

"What does she say?" Dad inquired. Bobbling my head from side to side, I replied, "She always says, 'This is a reading class, you can read something else, but you can't do anything else.'"

"Sounds like a good answer to me," he said. "Look, Son, there is no way around reading. To excel in an area, you have to practice. I have had to hone many skills that I didn't particularly enjoy. And trust me, it's hard, but the rewards are great." He paused. "You understand practicing your sport, right or wrong? When Coach B. Russell asks you to shoot twenty shots from the free throw line in front of the team, you don't ask him, 'Can I do something else?'"

"Dad, that's different, I already know how to read."

"You already know how to shoot a basket from the free throw line. Why do you keep doing it? Can you perhaps do it better? Can you score every time?"

His words made sense. Dad peered over the top of his glasses in his standard checkmate look. Except all the sense in the world would not change that I loved basketball and did not love reading.

"Okay, I get it," I told him. "I'll try harder.

Can you talk to Mom about this summer academy thing? I've gotta play basketball this summer. Everyone's expecting me to. The more I play, the better I'll get. I'm gonna play in the NBA one day."

Concerned, Dad sat up straighter in his chair. He rolled his newspaper into a tube. "You are aware of the odds, aren't you? Only three high school players – three players make it to the NBA out of every 10,000. That's point-zero-three percent. Son, tell me some- thing…"

"Please, please, Dad." I knew my whining would be interrupted, but I was going to give it a shot anyway.

"I'm sorry, Washington. What is your definition of reality?"

"It's what's real." Trivia question—I knew my answer wouldn't be enough.

"Exactly, and what is real?" Dad asked. "Uhh…" I mentally searched for a better answer.

"Repeat after me. Reality is the state of being true."

"Reality is the state of being true," I repeated.

"Only driveway and PlayStation basketball this summer. In fact, don't let me catch you without a book nearby or those will go, too. You hear me?"

"Yes, sir." I backed away from the den. Had he finished? I bounced the ball twice onto the glossy, brown, wooden floors. I kept waiting for him to change teams, make a new call, be the referee. Summer vacation couldn't get any worse.

"Hey, Son, I was thinking…" That was close.

For a moment I thought I would really have to run away from crazy town. I knew Dad would be more understanding.

I slowed my steps, holding my breath, and my ball tightly. I walked back into the room.

Dad was smiling now. "There's always a bright side," he said, "With no summer league ball, we won't have any conflicts for the family reunion next weekend. We can all go." He flicked out his newspaper and went back to reading.

Really? A bright side? Summer just got worse.

Chapter 3

I sat up in bed, hoping that this last week had just been a bad dream. My eyes landed on the neatly folded clothes stacked on top of my dresser.

My nightmare was just beginning.

Mom knocked once and peeked into the room. "Time to get up. We want to be on the road within the hour."

I groaned and laid there in my bed.

It wasn't until I heard Mom outside my door that I got up and made my way to the bathroom. I washed my face, and brushed my teeth. Then I carefully put on each item of clothing.

Fully dressed, I stared into the mirror. I stared longer than I ever remembered staring at myself before. I wasn't a bad kid. I could be doing a lot worse. Why couldn't they see that? I was not happy with my parents at all.

By the time I jogged downstairs, my parents had everything packed into our charcoal gray SUV. Steam rose from the grass at five that morning. Who would have believed it? Who would have believed I woke up before the sun with no basketball game to attend?

Before we left on any trip, my parents always asked me to wait on the porch while they secured the house. When I was little, I imagined they worried they might forget me. Now I understood this system was their traveling routine. I dribbled my ball between and under my legs.

Securing the house meant checking and locking the windows and doors, leaving notes for the neighbors, and setting timers for alarms and sprinklers.

By the time we reversed down the drive- way, they would always begin their quiz for each other. Did you mention this or that to the Freemans? Did you lock the back doors? Did you set the alarms?

I never remembered Mom or Dad saying, "No, honey, I forgot. Let's turn around." I liked this drill of theirs. They were a team— the other team.

The churning smells from the nearby coffee factory and the bakery mixed with the steam made me feel trapped in some weird gaming world. My team was scheduled to leave for San Antonio in an hour to go to the first tournament of the summer. I still couldn't believe I wasn't going. A chance to play in Memorial Madness was super important. And here I was going… to my father's lame family reunion.

Every time the ball hit the wood, I mouthed a word. *Bounce* - I, *bounce* - can't, *bounce* - believe, *bounce* - this. The ball dribbled faster. My mouth moved faster. For an entire week, I had done every single thing they'd asked me to do.

"Read for at least an hour every day." "Write a one-page report over what you read today."

"Use closed caption when you watch the television."

I did other stuff, too, not because I was in trouble, but because I wanted to. I hadn't even mentioned practice, because I didn't really miss the suicides.

Bounce-They, *bounce*-still, *bounce*-hadn't, *bounce*-changed, *bounce*-their, *bounce*-minds. This was so not fair.

Staring through the white wooden poles that closed in our porch from the sun baked jasmine bushes, I waited.

This is really happening. This is really happening.

What exactly was their point? I had to go to a family reunion as punishment. That should be a reward. It's not, but it could be. How does any of this even make sense?

Oh yeah, the punishment was summer school. Which didn't start until next week. So, technically I could have played in this one tournament. Mom had already paid the fees months earlier.

Fake Ms. Peake, who hated me, decided on the very last day of school that I didn't read well enough. She couldn't have picked an earlier time? All year I read well enough to pass. Ms. Peake should be the one getting punished. For being tardy with this information. For being a sucky teacher. How was reading even considered a real class?

My parents didn't even stand up for me, call the school's principal or anything. Instead, this was really happening. What could I say?

Mom neared the front door. I bounced the ball at full force to block out her humming. Did she feel even a little sad for ruining my entire life? Did Dad? He understood how important basket-ball was to me.

Chapter 4

❧

"Okay, Wash, load 'em up," Mom half whispered and half sang as she jetted past me. Wash? She was in a good mood. She had on road clothes - embarrassingly tight yoga pants, crazy rainbow colored Converse, and last year's Thompson family reunion t-shirt.

Dad came out next. He wore white tennis shoes, white ankle socks, below-the- knee pressed khaki shorts that didn't sag, and his last year's family reunion t-shirt that read Thompson Pride on both sides. He locked the front door. Whistling, he rushed for the car.

Whistling and humming? This sucked.

They really didn't care.

My first attempt to stand, failed.

We still had time–the team left in another hour,

right? Even though I'd missed a week of practice, I was sure that Coach B would let me play. I even wore my Monarchs' uniform with my new retro J's, mostly just to irritate Mom. But that made me ready just in case they changed their minds. I kept sitting on the porch, squeezing my ball.

"Wash, did you forget something? What's taking you so long? We don't want to travel during the heat of the day," Mom called from the driver's seat.

It was almost June in Texas. Which part of the day didn't include the heat? Eight a.m.? Eight p.m.? It apparently was now—at five o'clock in the morning.

I stood from the wooden white porch seat that matched the railing, picked up my backpack and checked it: game, comb, brand new phone, and a book.

After tossing in my ball, I climbed into the back seat. My opponents sat waiting, strapped under their seatbelts.

"Uh, you are probably going to say no..." I stretched the seatbelt down across my chest. *Click.*

"What is it, darling? Put on your seatbelt," Mom said.

Not mentioning that my seatbelt was already fastened, I continued. "Can I, uh, play in the Memorial Day Tournament? I know I messed up in reading this year. But when summer school starts next week I promise to work really hard. I enjoyed reading the books this week."

Neither Mom nor Dad had turned their heads.

"I can even read for two hours a day when we get back," I began to slow down. "Uh, we still have time to make it to the drop-off by six. Just this one game? Please."

"No." They answered together. I slouched in my seat.

"Did you tell Mrs. Freeman about the express package being delivered today?" Dad asked.

"I sure did. Oooh, did you set the lights to alternate with the sprinklers?" Mom asked.

"Check."

It seemed as if I hadn't asked the question at all. Mom drove right onto the highway. The numbers glowed from the clock.

Only twenty-three minutes later, Dad decided he wanted to get breakfast.

Mom took the next exit in search of food. I could have been on the bus with the team by now. I sulked while Mom pulled up to a fast food restaurant.

"Welcome to Gamble's. Order when you're ready," yawned a girl's voice into the car.

"I'll have pancakes and sausage. Honey?" Dad said.

"Two cheese and egg biscuits, with straw- berry marmalade. Wash, what will you be ordering, darling?"

"I'm not hungry, Mom."

"Suit yourself. That will be all for us this morning," she said.

Dad started to rant while the girl's voice still rambled from the speaker. "Robin, move up. Why would you order eggs on a road trip? You know I cannot tolerate the smell of eggs. We are in an enclosed area that will soon smell of rotting sulfur."

"You know what? When I'm stressed I crave eggs. Gallery business or rather the lack of, has me a little on edge. I'll let the windows down until the air clears or until I think of a minor business miracle. So, we won't have to ride back with the windows down." She twisted the AC to full blast.

She got him. One word about her struggling art gallery, and he left her alone. That made me sad. I remembered Mom's old art kiosk in the Galleria Mall. I stayed with her all day and watched the other people my age attached to their big people by long suitcase straps. They were everywhere. I don't see people with keep-up-with-your-child-connect- a-kid-strings much anymore.

We got a real gallery right after that. I grabbed my bag. I needed my game. The wiry headphones dangled from the sleek black hand held. I pushed the headphones into my ears and listened to the game's intro old school rap music to tune out my parents' conversation, "what to do about the failing gallery."

My pursed lips reflected from the shiny screen.

People travelled from everywhere to compare one new Black artist versus another. Photographs, sculptures, murals, drawings, and paintings packed the entire three level warehouse. Newspaper and magazine reporters interviewed Mom weekly for their feature stories.

Every week we hosted a new artist's opening. I loved the openings. Mom knew how to throw a party. The food always came from the same place, Fusion's House of Chicken and Waffles. Servers delivered huge silver pans to set atop tiny fires. After they positioned the last tray, Mom blasted a mix of jazz and house music. I stayed out of the way until I heard that blast of sound.

"Hit it!" she would grab my hands to twirl me around.

We danced. She pulled her arms up with her head flung back and pretended to play horns. I beat imaginary drums. Mom wore fancy black dresses on opening nights. Then one by one, guests would begin to arrive. We would settle down. This was our 'get hype' ritual. She used to be so cool.

I guessed I got too much into basketball. I didn't notice when the reporters and artists stopped coming. The art events just stopped.

I flipped on NCAA Live. Select. Select. Start. I could still play my game even as we sped toward East Texas to our boring family reunion.

Chapter 5

❧

When the air in the car changed from sooty to dusty, I knew the city was far behind. I popped out my headphones.

Horns and drums filled the warm car. Mom bopped her head as she lazily held the steering wheel with her left hand while Dad read one of his many books.

When we travelled to Henderson, where my father's family was from, I wondered if my dad thought about his dad, George Square. The last time anyone ever saw him was at a stupid family reunion.

I kind of remember that day and kind of not since I was only four years old when Grandpa George disappeared. He just went for a walk and never came back. He didn't quit his job coaching, pack his clothes, or even say good-bye. He just left.

Maybe Dad never wanted to miss a family reunion because he secretly hoped his dad would return. Maybe it was why my dad seemed sad most of the time.

Mom looked at me from the rear view mirror. "Wash, you joining us?" Her sparkly light brown skin shimmered under the sun.

Dad added, "Finally joining the living?

Who's playing that horn?"

"Uh… Dizzy Gillespie," I guessed. "That's my man." He beamed.

"No, that is my baby." Mom hated when Dad called me a man.

I didn't really know the answer. Dad drilled me on three different jazz muscians-Dizzy Gillespie, Thelonius Monk, and Charlie Parker. I guessed the right one. With a Black history question, the an-swer could have been one in a billion instead of one in three.

Dad pointed his chin to his shoulder and asked if I was hungry yet.

I shook my head. "Hunger strike."

"Let me know if you change your mind. I have some pancakes left." He returned to reading his open book, Between the World and Me. He had been reading that book for a few days. He carried it everywhere. The books he enjoyed he kept for a while. The books he didn't—I saw him with them once or twice, and then they went to their new home, a case in the den. I just didn't get it. That's what he wanted me to do. Read all of the time, but they couldn't force me to be like Dad.

I really didn't get it. There were more things to do besides read. Maybe when my parents were my age they didn't have choices–like games, or cell phones, or a billion television channels. Why did I need to read books? There were words to read everywhere. It's not like I was stupid.

Did they really think I wouldn't get into a good college? In the seventh grade, or was I technically still in the sixth? They had already given up on me. I played ball. I was not a nerd, or a blerd. I played basketball, and I was good—really good. And I will get into a great college just because of that. Maybe they didn't have anything that they loved like I love basketball.

I tilted my head to lean on the window and tried to sleep. The wind in the windows sounded like flapping falcons carrying the car to Henderson Hell.

When I woke up, the scenery had changed. Rows and rows of greenhouses filled with plants interrupted by giant pines followed rows and rows of green houses. We must be close. To the right, the green sign on a silver pole proved me right-Henderson 17 miles. I checked the clock.

9:52. Speed equalled the distance travelled divided by the time. I calculated that we would enter Henderson at 10:09. Dad taught me it took a minute to drive a highway mile at 60 mph. Whenever we passed distance signs, I figured out when we would enter the next town. I exchanged the comb from my backpack with the game. I straightened out my lop-sided Afro. Better I did it before Mom saw my hair. She showed no mercy with combing.

At exactly 10:09, the sign to the right read Henderson, Texas.

Chapter 6

❧

Our car slowed on the highway. The blinker's ticking blended with the dizzying jazz. Dad flipped down his visor and rubbed his face. We exited right into another world.

"My sweet gentlemen," Mom cleared her throat, "I have an announcement. When we return from this wonderful family retreat," she cleared again. "I am closing the gallery. Mr. Washington, I see you didn't read this morning. Find some time to read today, okay? I only ask for an hour a day."

Mom didn't give either of us a chance to respond. Instead she sealed the windows after she changed the subject to the subject I hated. She could have told me about the reading five hours ago. "Yes, Mom."

The bumpy dirt road reminded me that we

weren't in civilization anymore. The light shining through the car windows disappeared because of the giant trees overhead.

Mr. Purvis, my craziest of all time teacher, once taught our science class that the width of a tree trunk could be used to tell its age. During class he took us outside in front of the school. Using some string and a measuring tape, he found the circumference in inches of a tree from four and a half feet above the ground. I was the only one tall enough to help him. Mr. Purvis took out his calculator and rambled about finding the radius and dividing by ring width. "There, this tree is a baby. It registers at about 150 years old." After all of that we just went back inside and sat down.

If that little tree at school was 150 years old, these trees must be a million years old.

The road ended with a wide-open space. There it stood, the Hall. A porch wrapped around the huge, old, white, wooden house.

No part of the building touched the land. On every corner, a set of stairs led to the porch. Its red roof matched the red dirt.

The reunion festivities had already started.

Clusters of cars covered the splotchy lawn.

We parked.

Dust hung in the sun rays and masked everything, even the raggedy basketball goal on the half playground. Dusty, country, stuff everywhere.

I slung my backpack over one shoulder. Little kids circled us before my J's even touched the ground. At least fifty people were already there. And we arrived early.

My parents were excited; I could barely keep up with them. I liked seeing them happy, holding hands and rushing to see their friends and family. Mom enjoyed the reunions as much as Dad. They shared so many people. I guess that was because they had been together forever.

The Washington's, my mom's family, did- n't have reunions. They didn't have to—every other day was a festive affair. Half of them lived in Third Ward near us. Mom acted super young at dad's reunions like one of the girls at my school. It was kind of cute. I shadowed them through the maze of babies and cars into a sea of kin.

"Square, look how you've grown. Come give Momma Mae a hug," cackled a woman I swore I'd never seen before.

Why did every male's middle name in my family have to be Square? At home no one knew my middle name, but here, it was every- one's real name. Country, country, country.

"There he is—our very own basketball star," I heard some Square yell out.

Could you talk to my parents about that? I itched

to yell back.

Mustard greens, macaroni, casserole this, casserole that, rolls, fruit pies, cakes, salted watermelons, barbecue, fried chicken, and fruit salads—all sat wilting on the long tables bordering the Hall.

Someone forgot to tell these people that flies use the bathroom every time they land or at least about germs. I won't eat one disgusting bite.

After I used the bathroom, I was leaving. My parents couldn't punish me anymore. I was here, not playing basketball, needing to read a book. This super sucked.

"Come on over here, Square, give me five," hollered a man between clicking of the domino deal.

"Gotcha," he hollered again as he pulled his hand away.

My hand swam through air. I pretended to laugh with him.

"Hey, Dad, I need to go inside."

"Okay, we will be right here."

I jogged up the steps that lead to the white-screened front door. No one lived in the Hall; it was kind of a museum for the family. I loved the rooms. Each room had a theme.

The great room showed off family achievements. Before the family reunion, people included good news from the year with their fees. Aunt Ida hung them, like a blog. This time Aunt Ida posted some of my basketball clippings. The two side walls had an imaginary half split dedicated to the four children of Square. The left one was Hollis' and Delia's, the right wall - W.E.'s and Irvin's — our wall. I read ours.

A plastic covered newspaper article about Grandpa George was in the center. *A Houston family is desperately asking East Texas residents for their help in locating their missing family member. Hilton Thompson said the last time he saw his father, George Thompson, 51, was Saturday while he was at their family property in Henderson. County officials confirmed late Sunday that was the last known place the man was seen. Hilton Thompson and a host of family members were expecting George to return after a walk, but haven't spoken to him since 4 p.m. Saturday. "He went for a stroll, which he does daily and didn't return to the evening festivities," Hilton said. The man is described as being 5 feet 11 inches tall and weighing about 160 pounds with a thin build.*

He has black hair, brown eyes, and wears glasses for reading. Anyone with information on George Thompson's whereabouts is urged to contact county authorities at (409) 555- 5678.

What happened to my grandfather? That's just weird—his walking off like that.

Chapter 7

❧

In the center of the room, a braided red, yellow, black, and green rug covered the super shiny dark wooden floors.

It was silent.

I drifted into the room connected with the great room. Usually, I went straight to the dining area, because it was the war room. Framed soldiers of different family members decorated the walls. In a fancy cabinet, medals and weapons lined the shelves. Apparently a Thompson had served in every American war—the American Revolution, the Civil War, World War I and II, The Korean War, Vietnam, even the Wars in Afghanistan and Iraq.

Today, I went to my great-great-great grandfather's room. Light spilled in from the uncovered window. My dad said that Square died in this room on that bed. His wooden bed looked like a kid's bed, not a bed for the giant man that created our entire Thompson family.

I sat on the bed and gazed around the room. I made myself comfortable. Today would be a long day. Being on the bed felt powerful and weird at the same time. I stretched out on the bed of Square.

I'm being weird. I'm being really weird. Why am I here? It just didn't make a lot of sense. The family in Henderson didn't really seem like my family to me. Maybe if we lived closer. The people that were my age actually hung out together in their non-reunion time. They lived here. When I came, I was an outsider, the city kid.

Why did we have family reunions anyway? Like who invented them? None of my friends' families had reunions. Maybe everyone did. Maybe we just didn't talk about them.

I would just stay here, I decided. I could rest and read until someone made me leave. This is good a place as any.

His things, mostly old books including an ancient Bible, still lay on the dresser covered in plastic.

Square's giant painted picture, the same as the one at our house, glazed the wall. He still wasn't laughing. "What's up, Square?" I swore when I leaned to the left, his eyes moved with me, then again when I leaned to the right.

I raced from the room straight to the porch. The squeaky screen door slammed be- hind me. My heartbeat tapped fast and hard inside my chest.

I forgot to use the bathroom. That sucked.

About one hundred different Thompsons now stood facing an elder lady wearing a queen's crown made from silver and crystals. The bling and the sun caused sparkling glitter drops to shimmer over the crowd each time she moved her head.

They all burst into the "Black National Anthem."

"Lift ev'ry voice and sing, Till earth and heaven ring. Ring with the harmonies of Liberty; Let our rejoicing rise, High as the list'ning skies, let it resound loud as the rolling sea."

When they got to the booming 'sing a song' part, my insides collapsed. The song sounded awful. I sneaked down the stairs and searched for my escape.

Patches of giant trees grew behind the yard of the reunion hall. I casually walked in that direction without glancing back.

Chapter 8

❧

Leaning back against a giant tree trunk, I slid to the ground under towering East Texas trees. When staring up, light dots darted through loosely plaited branches.

I relaxed in silence far away from the Thompson comedy show. Rust-colored dirt covered my socks and shoes. I wondered when Mom would notice my disappearance. I should not have left. I reached into my back- pack to grab my game, and stopped. If I read, at least I would have an excuse for leaving. I grabbed the book instead.

I read.

I didn't know how long I had been reading *A Girl Called Boy* or what the story was really about, but my stomach growled. I had not eaten all day. I'd rather eat dirt than to return to the country circus and eat food of the flies.

Laughing, I cupped a handful of red dirt and licked it. It tasted sweet and crunchy like bits at the bottom of a Pop Rocks packet. I let the dirt crackle in my teeth. I squinched as I swallowed.

I wanted to stick out my tongue like a 'Double Dare' contestant, but something in the air had changed. This air looked photo filtered. I sat in the same place next to the same tree. I rubbed my eyes to try to rub the filter away. A cold finger touched my shoulder. A shiver ran through my body as if a Popsicle pushed onto my skin. Swatting at my arm where I felt the push, I stopped.

I tried not to move a muscle, not even my chest. Most everything looked the same except for the haze and that something or someone breathed heavily next to me. Something big. I just stared and stared and stared straight ahead still not moving. I began a visual search for my escape. My eyes jotted around in all directions.

There's no way I was going to sit here and do this. How could I run? How would I get away? Wouldn't that be weird to just jump up and start running? I mean this obviously wasn't happening for real. Maybe I was just tired. Maybe I was hungry. Maybe it was a bear. There were no bears here. It didn't poke me like a bear. Maybe I was in a mirage, but that happens in the desert. Maybe this was a forest mirage. That's it. I was just hearing breathing and feeling fingers, so why not just stay still and wait it out.

What's the worst that could happen? I guess ultimately I could go into shock and have a heart attack and die. This sucked.

A tall black man with wild hair, and deep scars on his cheeks leaned close to me.

Mom warned me to protect my brain be- cause it ran my entire body. That warning was the main reason she never let me seriously play football and any other extreme contact sports. She spoke a lot about Muhammad Ali when she went on a concussion rant. Mom scolded me after games for being too aggressive. I still managed to bang my head a few times—flying out. Alarm and panic swam through my mind. I must have hit my head too many times because I was definitely seeing things.

"Which Square are you?"

Chapter 9

❧

What the…I recognized him. Square, my great-great-great grandfather. *What's up, Square?* The question floated through my mind, but the words didn't travel out of my mouth because he was a person, and not a picture.

"Let me touch your face." He softly wiped his hand over my face. "One of Irvin's, same nose. Ate some dirt, did ya?" His smile spread into a grin, almost a laugh. "It's been a while. Well, let's have a talk."

He was real.

Dazed, I followed his lead. We leaned back on the base of the tree. Except for the blink of my super shocked eyes and the rise and fall of my chest with my hammering heart, I still sat completely still.

"Son, you not gonna speak? I'm Square Thompson, and this is my land. On occasion, one of you Squares comes for a spell. Who's your daddy?" He asked without looking in any direction.

"Hilton Square," I blurted.

"No, don't recall him. Who's his daddy?" "George Square," I answered.

"There's one I know. He's around these parts somewhere. George visited us all the time, couldn't stop eating dirt. He would bring plenty of books and hearsay. Then one day he up and decided to stay. Said living in two worlds just wasn't for him. He carried on about too much fighting or something of that sort."

Grandpa George stayed here. "Stay… stayed where?"

"Stayed back here with me and the old folks. And, by what do they call you?"

"Washington."

"Washington…Square?"

"Yes, Washington Square."

"Happen to have a book, Washington?" His soft, sad voice sounded like Dad's.

I pointed to the book on top of my bag. "Yeah, but I hate reading and reading hates me."

"Hold it right there," he interrupted. "Don't you ever form your lips to utter them words again. I see we need to taste a bit of this dirt together."

Square spat four times in front of him on- to the ground. He leaned over and clawed some clay from the earth. "Right now, do exactly what I do."

My mouth was dry. Sucking the sides of my cheek, I wanted to make a lot of spit, but I couldn't. I spit once, then again, then again and then again. What was I doing?

I scraped the ground the way he did. He rolled the red clay into a tiny ball between his middle finger and his thumb. I rolled mine into a ball.

He gently took my other hand and pulled me up while he stood. Square curled his arm and threw the dirt ball between his dark open lips. I hesitated for a moment and then did the same. I chewed the dirt the same as when I sat at the bottom of my tree, but this time afraid, I left my eyes open.

Like a basketball spinning on my fingertips the world around me began to move. Pictures swirled around me, then stopped like the scene selection on a DVD. First, Black books banned.

Tick-neighborhood cop shot hoodied teen. Starbursts.

Tick-Black people waded in waist high brown water holding misspelled signs pleading for help.

Tick-pretty brown girl in white with white bows walked with white suits up wide stairs.

Tick-newspapers burned.

Tick-workers bent in a field under a scorching

sun.

STOP.

The hairs on my body vibrated across my skin.

"Square, you okay, Son?" He laid eyes directly on me for the first time. He didn't have eyelashes or eyebrows, just eyes covered by wrinkles of skin.

The air smelled the same as my favorite cereal, Cinnamon Crunch Toasties.

Square breathed in deeply. He let his head roll back, which showed the bones in his throat, "You smell that, Son?"

"The lady folk mix all kinds of tree barks, herbs and leaves to make salves for the slaves to wear during the heat of the day. It's a beautiful sweet smell."

In his memory, could he read my mind?

My senses tipped off one by one.

Someone sang. No, people were singing.

"In these fields, I'll bury my soul. In these fields I'll bury my soul. In these fields, I'll bury my soul. No mo' way to get back home."

I saw them. Black men, Black women, and Black children. They wore all white with white wraps on their heads.

About forty of them folded over rows of corn and passed straw loads back to the ends like a step team. Their movements were definitely planned with dips, twirls and music.

"In these fields, I'll bury my soul. In these fields

I'll bury my soul. In these fields, I'll bury my soul. No mo' way to get back home."

They sounded even better than the choir from Emanuel A.M.E. When they got to the 'No mo' way to get back home' part a tall man with long dreadlocks yelled, "*Ebhochimbo*."

Then they started the same verse again. They advanced down the rows and kept in step – high stepping forward, mastering the crop.

"Oh, the sad songs that bind us," Square's voice interrupted the show. "So there are some rules by which you have to follow. A circle of bright clay dirt will be surroundin' our feet. The dirt glows right around my steps. You see it? Stay close by me because the ring protects me, 'cause it's my memory. You can step out of the ring to see them things I can't recall, but only for a day and a night. Only 'til that time you step out 'til that time comes round again, or else you'll be stuck forever in the past. You hear?"

"In the past? Uh, yes, sir," I answered. What's happening here? Where was I? Did

Square really just trick me? What the heck was he talking about? Stuck forever in the past? This really couldn't be happening. I couldn't be in the past. What did that even mean?

I'd been kidnapped. I tried to remember what to do if someone kidnapped you. I thought back to the human trafficking assembly from school this past year. Never go with the person. Too late for that. I was supposed to kick, run and scream. I couldn't kick an elder. What if I ran and he was telling the truth, and I got stuck? I'd like to get back to the reunion. Were those people over there-about to abduct me, and pay this Square look-a-like money for stealing me?

I screamed.

"Son, what are you doing? No one can hear you, but me."

I gulped in air and screamed again–this time louder.

None of those people noticed my cries for help. Who were they?

A red dirt ring burned brightly around our feet. It reminded me of my lucky hoop at home. Quickly, I bent over the ring. Was it hot? I wondered. Glowing dirt with its heat waves waved up from the ring and matched the steam from this morning's grass.

"Don't touch it, Son. We believe in movement around here in the memory. It's odd how it works. I'm still figuring out the trickery even after all this time. Your things can't go back in time but the things of the past can move forward. The real haints tell us that taking anything back to where you come from changes things. Changes the story, changes the reality. Taking anything-even a little speck of dirt."

People moved around the field.

"Them your people, your roots," Square said. "Aren't they fine? I can't see them yet, I'm not in this part of the memory."

What was he talking about–memory?

This was not quite how I pictured slavery. I had always imagined Black people running around naked, screaming, and crying. These people were strong and precise as if they were performing some half time drill show between periods.

Chapter 10

The singing abruptly stopped.

I heard someone riding on the horse be- fore I saw him. Did he belong in this memory? Sometimes at a league game one person accidentally sat on the wrong side in the bleachers. From the floor that one person stuck out. That's the tan man I saw now on the horse. He was white. He wore a white shirt, dark pants, and boots.

I faced Square. He squinted to adjust his eyes. He turned my chin and gently forced me to take in his memory.

The man finally rode into the scene. He drug and yanked on a rope. At the other end of the long rope I saw me. Me? That couldn't be me, because, I was here. This man had a keep-up-with-your-Square rope. I imagined them at the Galleria.

The horseman immediately began to yell. He pulled the rope in his hand and shook his free fist. "You see this here mid-day coon? In his restin' time he thinks he ought fancy books and readin'."

He pointed in the direction to where we stood. My stomach tightened into a knot and vomit pushed and burned into my mouth. I swallowed the vomit back down. It burned.

"I catched him over yonder in them trees with this here readin' book." He threw the book to the ground far away from him. "Now I want y'all to gather 'round."

Like sticky maple syrup the slaves moved slowly from where they stood and surrounded the man, the horse, and the boy. Some walked over the book, some split around it.

"Griffin, make me here a fire. Nothin' too big, don't want Mr. John a worryin'."

An older Black boy exited the group. He shook his head. Dust clouds powdered his feet as he scooted around the crowd.

"Coons need to fancy workin', an not readin'. Ya hear? Workin' hard for kind hearted Mr. John. That's all–jus workin'." He took the end of the rope and yanked Square toward him, almost lifting him from the ground. The man jumped down off the horse. "Readin' is fer whites, not fer coons. Ya hear?"

I couldn't see everything that was happening, but I could still hear everything.

Square grabbed my hand. He squeezed so hard, I felt my blood my stop running.

In the sky, the sun met a rope. It rose and fell and rose and fell and rose and fell.

Falackish... falackish... falackish.

The men slaves with their heads down scanned over the dirt. The women lifted their arms to the sky.

Falackish... falackish... falackish. Whipping sounds slapped in the air.

"Ebhochimbo," shouted the man with the dreadlocks.

Another man from outside of the crowd looked at me. He peered deep into my eyes. My heart thumped faster and faster. I shook all over. Stair number one... stair number one. It was Grandpa George. George Square Thompson, my dad's dad.

Falackish... falackish... falackish.

Ebhochimbo.

Chapter 11

❧

Square's memory faded and now I only saw Grandpa George. He wore the same gear as the other men slaves—thin white saggy pants and a loose fitting white shirt. He appeared to have more red dirt splotches sprayed on his clothes than the other men.

Grandpa George stared our way. Could he see us? I waved.

He didn't wave back. He glared.

The movement of my hand caught Square's attention. "They can't see you, but some of the time, I think some of them can feel you."

Grandpa George squatted next to the book. He didn't look much like my dad, but moved his body the same. As he looked at the book, he raised his eyebrows, which caused lines to ripple in his forehead. The next moment he relaxed and the lines disappeared. He twisted his lips from side to side. He was thinking. Dad did that when he thought, too.

I wanted to meet my grandfather. I wanted him to see me.

The bright circle on the ground grounded me firm to where I stood, because the image of slavery, or living in slavery, or staying in slavery scared me. Like really scared me.

It hit me. Dad had possibly noticed that I was missing. Vanished, just like Grandpa George. "I'm still okay. Dad, don't worry. I'll be back," I whispered.

If he had really noticed, he was freaking out on the inside. Dad probably wouldn't tell Mom, because she freaked out on the outside, big time.

At the reunion, Rites of Passage drills happened after dinner. Really it was lunch, but everybody around the land called it dinner.

The boys went with the men, the Squares, the girls went with the women. We all learned stuff. Sometimes we watched African films, or African-American movies. We recited our family tree in the unity circle. It seemed someone could have mentioned this at some point during Rites—this whole incident, Square was beat for reading. Maybe they did, I didn't always listen.

We learned words in Swahili. Dad taught the

Swahili. I listened to him. This year he also planned to announce the family's DNA testing results from last year's spit samples.

Search parties and prayer circles probably replaced regularly scheduled events: line dancing, domino tournaments and scholarship awards.

A breeze lifted the cover of the book. How could anyone want to read a book that badly? What was in it? There wasn't a book in the world I would read if I knew I'd get into this kind of punishment for it. Even if it had all of the answers to all of the homework I would ever get forever. I wouldn't read it. What was in that book? Maybe it made people love to read or made them crazy. Maybe both. Grandpa George bent and looked like he was drawing in the dirt. He spat, he spat, he spat, and he spat. With his first two fingers and his thumb he rolled a ball.

Grandpa George looked our way again. Square didn't seemed to notice Grandpa George. I guessed he wasn't a part of Square's memory. The only way he could be here was if he stepped out of the circle, and didn't make it back in a day…right? Why would he do that? Why would anyone stay here?

Chapter 12

❧

Square squirmed away, but he still watched the scene of his memory.

The slaves crumpled to the ground, crying. I could finally see the white man and the Boy Square again.

This white man pulled a metal wand from the fire near his feet. What was he going to do with that? As soon as the question popped into my head, he did it. He stuck the wand near Square's eye. Then the man pressed the wand into the Boy Square's face. He pressed and pressed.

Did I just see that? He just burned Square's eye! How could he do that? First, he beat Square, now he burned one of his eyes. For reading a stupid book? Okay, this was not a movie. This was not a television show. This was not a game. This was insane.

A shudder bounced around my body. Clutching my stomach, I wanted to throw up. I squinted enough to keep watching the hor- ror show through my eyelashes.

This was what Mom meant—my ancestors lost their lives for my right to read. Lost their lives, okay. But got their eyes burned with hot metal? She left out that part.

Square's body began to tremble. I wondered how many times he remembered this day.

"That's how I got our land, Son. When Missus seent me, she never did forgive her- self. She's the one who gave me the reader to start with. She left all the land to me after Mister John died. Not even a little for her own people. She left it all to us." He sucked his teeth. "She even let me be free. I share cropped for a time. Then I bought my wife out. And that dear woman read to me every single day, mostly the Bible. She say she learned herself reading this very day my eyes got singed."

Not until after the branding of Square's second eye, did I smell the burning skin or hear the screaming. The screams of Square, my great-great-great grandfather.

The slaves, like me, were stunned into silence.

A small puddle pooled between my sneakers. Was I wetting my pants? I was wetting my pants. I heard it, I smelled it, and I didn't care.

I faced Square. The top of my Afro met the top of his head. We were almost the same height. I waved a hand in front of his golden brown face. "Can you see?"

"Only in my memory, only before this moment in my past."

I felt it. I was about to Fly Out of Bounds.

I shook my head like a wet dog. Grandpa George kept folding and unfolding, then refolding his arms. He flew way out of bounds when he decided to stay here and deal with this. Deal with slavery.

Between one of his arm crossings, he paused and kicked dirt over the cover of the book that still lay on the ground. I hoped he won't pick it up. What if another slave picked it up? Was that what the white man wanted? Was that why he threw it on the ground in the first place?

The lines of everything began to blur. My breaths were short and loud. I squeezed my eyes so tight static dots ricocheted behind my eyelids. I had to stop Square's memory from sinking into my brain. I tensed and squeezed my whole body tight. I froze.

Dad's voice echoed from the place where Square's memory floated. A blanket of peace covered me.

Reality is the state of being true.
Reality is the state of being true.
Reality is the state of being true.

I wanted that book. I thought I did. I hat- ed reading and reading hated me. I needed that book. I had to get it so no one else in my family got hurt because of it. At least I could do that. My parents would want me to get the book.

Reality is the state of being true.
Reality is the state of being true.
Reality is the state of being true.

Suddenly, I felt like I was in the mural "Family Unity" painted on the ceiling of our house. This was the other side of backward in the spiral tree trunks with those kids.

Reality is the state of being true.
Reality is the state of being true.
Reality is the state of being true.

This was reality.

Chapter 13

❧

I opened my eyes and stepped one foot out of the ring. Now the other. Left foot. Right foot. Left foot. Right foot. I took in a mouthful of dusty air. Shaky fear filled my body. I was afraid.

To keep focused I talked with Coach B in my head. "What's the plan, Coach?"

"We don't have one for this game." "No really, what's the plan, Coach?"

"Same as always…get the ball. Take it to the hole. Mind the clock. Remember, keep your eye on the clock."

Immediately, I pictured a shot clock. It was extended from a floating tripod. The red dots danced on the black screen bordered in white. The dots froze as the numbers read: *23:59 freeze, 23:58 freeze*.

Where was Square? I pivoted on my heels. Sharp shooting sun rays replaced where I stood with Square just two minutes before. I couldn't see Square. He's gone. I couldn't see the ring. How would I get back? Sweat covered my hands. I twisted them around each other. They slipped apart.

Okay, I had officially flown out of bounds. This was not like knocking that idiot in his head with a rubber ball. This was like, I was going to be a slave forever because I hated reading.

I took a step back.

Get the book… take it to the hole. But now there wasn't a hole.

I took another step back.

Get the book… take it to the sun. Watch the clock.

One more backward step.

Get the book… take it to the sun. *Watch the clock. 23:26 freeze, 23:25 freeze.*

I had done this before. I could run back court and back in no time at all. I needed to spin around.

I did.

The white man shouted while waving away the workers. "Gemini, go wrap up this boy. Y'all get on back to work. Hope today ya learned something." He pet his horse like it was a giant cat. He mounted his giant kitty and left just as quickly as he entered the scene. The slaves waited a millisecond, suspended and then they came alive. When you drew a chalk line in front of a parade of ants, they forgot about order and shot in all directions. The slaves were like that; they scattered like confused ants.

I pressed full speed toward the book. This wasn't as easy as I thought. Now that people staggered around the book and over it.

One lady collapsed flat to the ground. "Why? Why? Why?" She yelled the same word over and over. She waved away people that looked like they were trying to help her.

I slowed to a jog. Could that be my great-great-great-great grandmother?

A half of a wet hiccough burned inside my neck as a warm shower of air sprayed around me. It's fear and love all at once, for these people, my people. I stopped, curious to see her face. Had I ever seen that face? Did any pictures of her hang at the stairs or in the Hall?

The sun baked the back of my body. The sun. Thinking of the sun made me think of the make believe shot clock: *23:15 freeze 23:14 freeze 23:13 freeze 23:12.*

Two tiny girls saw me. So did everyone else —even the woman crying on the ground looked at me. I studied her bronze freckled face. Behind tears and her deep creases, she was very beautiful and looked very young. They could definitely see me. I sucked in a long, dusty breath. I breathed out and lowered my chin to the top of my chest.

What the… where were my clothes? I was naked. Naked. No jersey. No shorts. No socks. No J's. No underwear. Naked.

Your things can't go back in time but the things of the past can move forward.

My whole body quit. My muscles ceased flinching, my heart slowed beating, and my eyes stopped blinking.

Chapter 14

A small group of men slaves continued to focus in my direction. Their gaze was harsh. Their blank, black faces probed mine. Were they mad, sad, scared, or curious? I didn't want to find out. I advanced quickly toward the book.

The cinnamon smell wrapped around me. Their silence and their stillness were like pages in picture books.

I looked like Square. This probably freaked them out. We all saw what happened to Square.

One person resumed motion. A slave girl marched straight toward me. I marched back. She was beautiful, beautiful like Imani. Her white costume made her angelic. She bounced so hard that her two side ponytails fluttered around her sepia face like wings. I was dead. I left the dirt ring and died. Square said I had a whole day. And still the angel of death walked to me to escort me to heaven.

My legs shook uncontrollably. I continued. She would have to take me with that book.

Suddenly, my angel squatted. Her eyes landed on the faces of certain slaves, respectfully seeming to ask a question. Some of them nodded. She snapped up the book and stuck it deep into the folds of her flowing skirt. Pointing away from the fields, the girl spun to run.

Really? Now, I had to follow her.

Where's Grandpa George? Maybe he could help. I needed to search for him later. I couldn't lose her. She had the book. My calves hurt. I had been tiptoeing for I don't know how long. I lowered my heels to the ground. The shaking started again.

I tracked her direction. I didn't have to go far. Next to a giant evergreen outside the cornfields, she sat. She had opened the book to the first page. She studied it with her eyebrows scrunched. The girl didn't even glance upward when I arrived.

"Are you crazy or something? Didn't you just see what happened to that boy for having that book? Aren't you scared?"

"I ain't scared of no haints. You can't do nothing to me. Shoo, I says. Shoo!" She swung her entire arm in my direction.

"What's a haint?"

"It's what you is. You probably hadn't figured it out yet. Square, remember when folks die and they ain't ready, they keep a wanderin' 'till they vanish. Square, you a haint now."

"I'm not Square. I'm not a haint." I spoke extra slowly. "My name is Washington and I came from a future time to get that book you are holding."

"Well, if you real, you better cover yourself," she said as she put one hand under her skirt. Lifting one hip then the other, she pulled down some pants that she wore underneath her skirt. "I'm Lucy and I still thinks you a haint, a confused haint at that."

"Okay, Lucy, whatever. Can I have the book?" I circled around the tree to put on the pants. I circled back around to face her.

"Naw, you can't have this book. I the only one not a feared to get the book. It's mine now. I gointa teach myself to read."

"Look, Lucy, you can't teach yourself to read. And I need that book. I need it now. Surely there's another book-"

"I can teach myself. Ask anybody. I'm the fastest learner. If I see it, I can remember it. Remembering everything is my gift."

"Your gift? I don't have time to listen to this. I've got to get back to those trees." I lunged to make the steal. Her fingers clasped tightly around both sides of the book. *Good offense.*

"You want me to start yellin' and hollerin'? I will. An ain't nobody gointa believe you not a haint and that you a boy named Washington."

"No. No, I just want you to give me the book."

This pretty, angel, slave, girl was mean.

Water bubbled in my eyes, then tears sprung everywhere. I didn't have time to slap my eyes to stop them. I finally cried for what I'd seen, where I was, who I was with and not with, and how I got here—here. I bent over. My chest quaked. Dust peppered the inside of my nose.

I started sneezing back to back. I couldn't stop either the crying or the sneezing. This had to be a nervous breakdown. Salty tears mixed with even saltier snot that both leaked into the corners of my mouth.

Lucy patted my back. I wanted to push them away. I wanted to push Lucy's hands. Her dusty bare feet on the ground were all that I saw.

"Now. Now. I don't think haints s'posed to cry like that. What you want again?"

"I'm. . ." I caught my breath in drowning gasps of air, "never…" gasp, "getting…" gasp, "back."

"Back where?"

"Haven't you been listening? You are crazy. My name is Washington. I'm from the future. I came to this time with one of my great grandfathers by eating dirt. I left our circle, to get the book, that book. I only have a day, one day, to get back to the circle or the trees or wherever I was. Or I'm going to be stuck here with you in slavery forever."

"You's not a slave boy? Why don't you just go back? I seent where you came from. And I seent where the sun was when you came. I seent it, so I remember. My gift. I'll take you to your circle. Why you gotta take my book? Can you read?"

My mouth and throat were now dry. I choked out the words. "Yes, but I HATE READING." This time I meant that for real.

She's right. I didn't need that stupid book.

I needed to get back to Square. What did I care if they all got beat and all their eyes burned out?

She looked like I had shouted a million curse words at her. Her tiny brown face tilted side to side before she began to speak.

"You the crazy one. Hates reading." Lucy shook the now closed brown book in my direction. "Reading's the only way that's gointa get us free. Keep all that hollerin' and that baby cryin' and you gointa be found fo' sure. And me too for that matters."

"You're right, Lucy. I'm sorry. Just take me back to where you saw me come into your world."

"I can take you back, but not now. It's time for

shift change. Driver's comin' back. We gotta get back on the field. You stay by me."

"Who is Driver? That's the white guy from before? On the horse?"

She didn't answer.

The pain of fear prickled then raced through my hands and feet. I was in slavery. "He's coming back?"

Chapter 15

❧

Lucy craned her neck over her left shoulder. She shushed me with a finger to her mouth. We listened for something, I didn't know exactly what.

"Okay, now," she ordered.

We skipped. Well, she skipped. I ran after her straight into a group of slaves leaving the fields. We sneaked into line.

They hummed a sad verse. Square's earlier description sprayed through my thoughts, *the sad songs that bind us.* I guessed this song was for Square's eyes.

The slaves stayed their distance from me. Most of them probably also believed I was a haint. I kept my eyes on Lucy and did exactly what she did. If she stepped, I stepped. If she stood, so did I.

When I finally saw the driver leading the line

riding his horse, sweat sprouted all over me. What if he saw me? I was the only one not wearing a shirt. What would I say? What would I do? I would run. He stopped.

I tripped and slammed into an older lady. Did the driver see me? What's he doing? He looked like he was counting heads and herding cows. Lucy gave me that look. The same look as before. She really believed I was crazy. Our group drug past him.

"See y'all come morning. Not nearly enough bags were filled today. That'll cost you double tomorrow."

No one talked to anyone for a while. We walked down a red dusty road. What the… that's the Hall, our Hall before it was our Hall. That was not my Hall. Two white women dressed in long layers and layers of white like us, but not like us, sat on the porch. Their white was lacy. They sipped from teacups.

White kids our age played in the yard passing a ball. One missed the catch; the ball rolled. It stopped next to the fence post that I would be passing in a second. I wondered what would happen if I grabbed it, spun it, bounced it, and threw it in the air back to them.

That would make life better. A ball in my hands. But right now, I was not free. I was a slave.

I followed Lucy. If she stepped, I stepped.

There wasn't a fence around our Hall now. Everything else looked pretty much the same. I bet it's the first thing Square removed. The fence separated their world from us. I felt invisible more than when I huddled with Square in the dirt ring.

Grasshoppers screeched in gaps that reminded me of the referees' whistles during a game.

Lincoln Logs. Life-size Lincoln Logs. Two rows of them. Two, four, six, eight, ten, twelve. I could see twelve from here. Mom and I used to build with miniature logs at the gallery. I pretended we made a city. It didn't matter which famous artist had an exhibit on display or what opening was scheduled for the day, no one could destroy our creation.

The field hands finally relaxed. They talked with one another. This must be home.

Where was Grandpa George? None of the men looked familiar. I guessed he went another direction when I copied Lucy's movements and I didn't notice.

He knew I was not a ghost. Maybe that's just what he did…disappeared when you needed him.

Chapter 16

We stopped at the third cabin on the left. Brushing by a potted plant that sat on the ground next to the door, an older woman entered just before we did. She left the door open. Lucy pulled me into the space. I nearly hit my head on clanging charms swinging from strings attached to the top of the door frame.

"Girl, you's ain't 'bout to bring no haints around here." The woman's glare sent chills all over me. Her black wrinkled face hid that it had ever smiled. "Shoo! Shoo now!" she hollered.

I froze. She was almost scarier than the overseer. Almost. Maybe she's the haint.

"Mama Tommi, he's no haint. He's a runaway. He run away to find his people." She didn't take a breath. She just kept lying. "Someone from the next fields over told him that the coloreds over here look like him. So, he sneaked away for the day to see what he could see." Amazingly, she didn't compute on her expressionless face at all. She had a game face.

"Is that true, boy?" Mama Tommi asked.

"Yes, ma'am," I answered. Here was my chance. "Ma'am, do you know of anyone named George on this land?"

She cocked her head to the side as if she knew something. "I understand. No, there is no person by that name round here, but you look an awful lot like Square and his mama. Shame what happened to her boy today. Shame what happens round here every day." Mama Tommi stopped talking just to shake her head. "I'm a go to cookin' and checkin' on things. While I's down there, I'll let everyone know who you is. 'Cause everybody gointa think we lettin' haints set in the quarters. And ain't nobody gointa see Square 'till least morning. That's if he be livin'."

Just like that Lucy started her chatter again. I paid extra close attention, so I could keep up with her story.

"Mama Tommi, this runaway's named Washington. He can read. And tonight he's gointa teach me reading." Never changing her game face, she twisted away from Mama Tommi to smirk at me. "You always say, reading's the only way that gointa get us free."

What was this crazy girl talking about?

"I thought he was searching for his folks—"

"He gointa look on the fields come mornin'. Tonight he's gointa teach me readin'."

"Not before y'all do the work that needs to be done around here. If he can read, I know Washington knows the work of the quarters?"

I didn't understand her question, but I understood she wanted an answer. "Yes, ma'am," I said, still thinking about what Lucy said I was going to do for her.

Looking satisfied, she continued, "I'll bring y'all some likker." Mama Tommi left out the front door, the only door.

As soon as I assumed she was far enough away, I exploded. "What the heck are you talking about? If I remember correctly, you said you could teach yourself to read. You are the fastest learner around here. Your gift, remember?"

"Remember? Remember you need to get back to your trees. Remember that you don't know the first thing 'bout 'round here. You don't even know how to walk right in front of driver. Washington, who is not a haint, we need each other. That's how we do here. You are gointa show me reading tonight." She grabbed a stick with corn husks tied on one end. "I've gotta go to the garden before moonrise and pick food for tomorrow. You need to sweep these floors and tidy." With that she threw me the stick, and left me all alone.

Each new sound from the other side of the wall freaked me out. *Thadck... thadck... thadck.* I peered between the slats and saw two men chopping wood.

Kids my age plucked vegetables from tiny gardens. Tomatoes and peppers in one gar- den, squashes–yellow, green and white in another. Lines of leafy greens, peas, onions, okra–the entire grocery store grew between and around these cabins.

I followed the walls of the cabin using my fingers as my guide round and round looking out into a surprising world. Five women gathered around two giant pots on fire fixing food. In door fronts, older women sewed. Itty bitty kids picked at cotton balls sat near these women's feet.

Thadck...thadck...thadck.

Didn't they just get back from work? They worked even harder than they did earlier in the fields. They worked together.

"Ouch." A sliver of wood stuck straight out my middle finger and disrupted this slave life reality show. A drop of blood seeped out around the splinter. This sucked.

I was being held hostage by Lucy, the crazy slave girl. She expected me to teach her to read tonight. This family reunion kept getting better and better. Had my parents just let me go to my basketball tournament, none of this would have happened. It's their fault they may never see their only child again.

Grandpa George probably didn't like to read either. I didn't know much about my grandfather. He was a good basketball player. He played in college and then professional ball for a few seasons. He was a college basketball coach. So, he was probably like me.

There was nothing to clean. They barely had anything in the first place. Lucy and Mama Tommi must have made everything in this room from some part of corn.

I wished I had my ball. Could I make one from corn? I started sweeping, sweeping around cornhusk stuffed bed mats, corn-thatched table and chairs, corn boxes. Corn boxes? Maybe, I could make a ball from corn.

Who swept dirt floors? Mom would.

I missed Mom. Surely by now she had noticed that I was gone. She was probably super worried.

I was so into basketball by the time I even noticed that the gallery only opened on Fridays and Saturdays. Mom stayed at home during the week. When I got home from practice on most days, she would be pacing around with her phone talking to investors or banks.

When she stopped pacing and began cleaning the floors, I started to miss the gallery. Mom did the floors. Floors, I knew that had already been cleaned. She polished the stairs constantly. She filled and emptied buckets of water mixed with sour lemon oil soap. Even after I went to bed, I heard the humming of the vacuum cleaner. I started to miss Mom, too. I wished I knew how to help her. After all it was our gallery.

That's when she started tripping about grades and school. "Washington, you need to be better than your competition. There is always room for improvement. Because there is always competition." I didn't know if she was talking to me or to herself.

Out of breath, Lucy burst into the room, snatching me out of my thoughts. "I'm finished. You?"

A pink and orange sunset glowed behind her. She had her skirt pulled up and stuffed with vegetables. It overflowed with okra, tomatoes, peppers, and onions. Lucy gently dumped the rainbow into a crate that sat beside the entrance. She looked like my angel again.

Thank God, she's back.

The door swung closed behind her. Lucy raced to the sleep area and pulled the book from under one of the mats. "The food's comin'." She smiled a perfect smile. "Let's read."

Chapter 17

Okay, what do I do first? I don't know. I just know how to read, like I've always known. We sat at the table and opened the book. Each letter of the alphabet was capitalized in fancy cursive on the first page. On the second were the little letters.

"These are the alphabets. Say 'A'." I hoped this would make sense.

"I know that. I can sing the whole song." She traced the words and sang. "'*A-B-C-D-E-F-G, H-I-J-K-LMNOP, Q-R-S, T-U-V, W—X—Y- and-Z, Now I know my ABC's next time-'* What do they mean? How do they work?"

The alphabet song was ancient? Now what? That was what I was going to teach her, but she already knows the song.

Her stare burned through the side of my

cheek.

"Well, they each make their own sounds. Yeah, each one of those letters make a different sound. Then you put them all together."

She was a frozen sculpture.

"When you put them together they make words. Then the words talk like we talk," I finished explaining.

She was back to computing. I had to figure this out to get out of this mess. She started to hum the song. This was worse than talking to a baby.

"Not the song sounds; the letters have sounds." Oh, yeah the vowels. "Some letters, the vowels, have two sounds. This letter is a vowel." I pointed to a letter in the book. "The first sound it makes is like its name- 'A'. The other is aah. Say aah."

With eyes squinted she made the animal sound of a goat. Did she even hear what I said? The shaking of my head let her know she was not even close. "Try, again. Aaaah."

Lucy gurgled spit in the back of her throat that ended in a ripple of 'R"s.

The fastest learner around? I was in big trouble. "No, aah. Put your finger on your tongue and make this sound." My finger pressed hard on my tongue to show her. I leaned forward.

She stuck her finger so far down her throat, she gagged. Was she going to throw up? If she did, it would be all over me.

I could see the pink insides of her esophagus. This was the closest I'd ever been to kissing a girl. She smelled like cinnamon sun. I wanted to kiss her. Weird.

"What y'all doing?" Mama Tommi stood in horror with a bowl in each hand. She walked to the table and slung down both bowls. Dark red sauce slopped over the sides.

"I's learning reading." Lucy leaned back and used an innocent voice she must only use with Mama Tommi.

"That's not what it be looking like. Where did you say you come from, boy?"

"He's from down the way, Mama. This likker sure looks good. I'll get the spoons."

"I's got some mending to do before morning. I's going across the way, but I'll be back. You hear?"

"Yes ma'am," we sang.

When the door closed, we burst out laughing. This was our first real laugh together.

Lucy passed me a spoon.

The soup was the best soup I'd ever had. It was filled with all of those garden collections. I was not a big fan of vegetable soup.

"Lucy, where are your parents? Is Mama Tommi your mother?"

"No, silly. Mama Tommi is my mama's mama.

My mama works in the big house. Like Mama Tommi did. Like I will one day. I sup- pose. My mama stay there. Sometimes she come and see me—bring me food from there.

She don't come much—just on holidays and big celebrations. I heerd my Papa went to an- other field to work. I don't know…"

A lump rose in my throat making it hard to swallow, and stinging returned to my eyelids. That's ridiculous—just seeing your mother on special occasions, your dad leaving to work and live somewhere else? I mean, I got it. Around here, you got beat, but I didn't think my dad would ever just leave me. Especially, after Grandpa left him. Maybe the other field owners bought her dad. Maybe he's not even alive.

She sounded so normal about it all. Possibly, it was normal.

I sometimes got upset with my parents, but I know I couldn't survive without them. I didn't want to. I missed them both even now–especially now.

Awkwardly, I changed the subject. "Uh, what kind of soup is this?"

At the same moment that I asked that question, Lucy started pressing the back of her spoon to her tongue.

From her mouth flowed the perfect sound for the short letter 'A'. "Aaaaaaah"

"Lu, you did it. That's it!"

"That's not my name. My name is Lucy Ann, not Lu." She concentrated again. "Aaaah," "A is 'A' and 'aaah'?" She forgot about dinner.

"A is 'A' and 'aaah'."

"Are you going to eat the rest of your soup?" I slurped the rest of the liquid from my bowl.

"A is 'A' and 'aaah'." No, I don't want any more. You had better hurry up, too. You got to learn me. A is 'A' and 'aaah'."

Red grainy spices settled at the bottom of the bowl. That's probably what made the soup taste so good. The spices. "What's this?" I asked, pointing into the bowl.

"Dirt, for the Dirt Likker. Washington you sure is fool."

"You eat dirt?"

"Dirt's the special spice. It's good for you."

I grabbed her bowl this time without the spoon and started drinking, wondering would the tasty liquid take me back to my time–take me home.

Chapter 18

❧

"Washington, is there an 'A' in my name?"

"In Lucy?"

"No, in Ann?"

"Yeah, Aaann, let me spell."

She jerked back at the word spell. "'A'- 'N'- 'N', Aaann."

Lucy kept repeating the spelling as a song. She sashayed around the table singing while holding our dinner bowls. After removing them completely from the cabin, she returned with a lit match. The flicker from the flame danced in her eyes. From beneath the table she pulled out a candle and lit it.

A day and a night. It's night time, and I was running out of time. I could teach her to read. Without words we began again.

Lucy traced her fingers over the letters, staring at each one at a time. Then she closed her eyes, shook her head, opened eyes, and traced again. "Tell me the sounds," she ordered.

"The next letter is 'B'. It sounds like-"

"Tell me the sounds just the sounds that the letters make."

"Buh… buh."

"Tell me all of them, fast."

I took the book from her hands and ran down the list. If this was how she believed, we should do this she was a lunatic. It took people years to learn the sounds of the alphabet. Insane. I didn't look up. I ran through the letters as fast as I could, saying the sounds of each letter from A to Z.

"There, now let's learn them the right way. We don't have a lot of time for this."

"Again, do it again." Lucy rocked back and forth. Her eyes flickered wildly back and forth. She repeated what I said after a small delay.

"Aah, buh, cuh, duh, eeh, fff…" I air bounced a ball with my left hand and followed the letters with my right.

"…Aah, buh, cuh, duh, eeh, fff." She rocked side to side.

"Mmm, nnn, aww, puh, quuh…"

"… Mmm, nnn, aww, puh, quuh."

"Errr, sss, tuh, uuh, vvuh, wuh, ixs, yah, zzzz."

"… Errr, sss, tuh, uuh, vvuh, wuh, ixs, yah, zzzz."

The light skipped around the dark room. The alpha chant that we rapped made me feel like we had landed in a movie where witches cast spells with wax dolls and hair of monkey legs. After minutes, she sang her new song-the alphabet sound song.

"What are you doing?" She pointed, noticing my bouncing hand.

She had stopped our game so quickly that it startled me.

I threw an air shot toward the door. "I'm playing basketball. It's the way I know how to win. Let's try some words."

I found random words that would be easy to pronounce.

Now, I finally remembered that Mom taught me to read this way. She sat next to me with little square books. They came in boxes that had a handle. The books each had a short story made with similar words. There were words like cat, rat, and dog. She guided me through them until I could read them on my own. She struggled with me on each one. She celebrated, too. This is how I would try to teach Lucy.

Lucy sounded out, repeated, and recorded the words in her brain using her crazy shake-her-head way. Her gift. Time seemed suspended.

I struggled and celebrated with her at the candle lit table inside the life-sized log cabin. Her eyes brightened when she mastered a new word. My chest inflated waiting for her to get through the next word. When she did, I exhaled. We were ready for sentences. She was the fastest learner. Half-time.

I really wanted to go search for my grandfather.

Chapter 19

"Put it away. Put that book up! Hide that boy! Marsa's checkin' through." Mama Tommi panted out of breath, running into the room. "Put it up, I said, now."

"He can't do nothing to me now. I's free now. I can read."

"Girlchild, did you see Square? Did you see what they done today?" Mama braced Lucy's shoulders.

"Him be tryin' to read. But, I can read. Readin's the only way that's gointa get us free. I's free."

"Looky here, boy, you gots no time and no place to hide. Get on that sleepin' mat. Face that there wall and play possum sleep. Don't you dare move. Or you's won't make it back up the road to where you came from. You hear?"

"Yes ma'am,"

"Hide this with you." She hurled the book in my direction.

Lucy kept repeating the words. Now she was singing them, too.

"If something happens to my girlchild, I'll kill you dead." Mama Tommi's whispering threat ended abruptly.

I fell to the mat.

The light tapping on the door echoed in my mind like crowds stomping on wooden bleachers. I imagined gray boulders flying off cliffs and crashing into rocky ledges. But, that was the pounding of my heart.

"How are you doing this fine evening, Tommi Jean?"

It sounded like a different voice from the crazy man earlier on the fields. I couldn't tell for sure because Lucy wouldn't stop with her word calling.

"Fat, cat, rat, mat, hat, sat, at, fat…"

"Fine, Sir, quite fine. What brings you through? Trouble, Sir?"

The hard thud of his boots moved closer to me then stopped.

"No, no Tommi, just wanted to walk the moonlight workers home for a change. What's the problem with the girl?"

"Dog, hog, log, fog, jog, hog…"

"Fits, I guess, Sir. It was a mighty hot today."

"My children practice rhyming when they learn to read..."

Tommi laughed nervously. "Oh yeah? Why I'm sure that's not Lucy's problem. Just fits, that's all. Fits, I say. Lucy, stop that nonsense and speak to Marsa John. He come to bid us a fine evening."

Lucy stopped.

I didn't hear anything-

"Pan, ran, can, fan, tan, ban..."

"Tommi, don't your people have some medicine or remedy for that type of behavior around here?" He circled toward me. "Now that's a good one. Sleeping before a long day's work."

The thud of his boots rested so close to me I could smell him. I smelled the mud on his boots, the grass from the fields, and the smoke from the cigar he must be smoking right now. Mmmn, an ash fluttered on my arm. It seared my skin. *Stay still, perfectly still.*

Don't move. I want to go home. I do.

I popped my eyes open, still facing the wall. I saw green—pure green. The pine wall was green. I couldn't fly out of bounds now. Couldn't fly out. I felt my arm flinch. I balled my hands into tight fists. He'd better not touch her. He'd better not touch her.

"Sit, fit, lit, hit, bit..."

Lucy shut-up. Shut-up, shut-up, shut-up!

"Yeah, that's a good one. *Early to bed, early to rise, makes a man healthy, wealthy, and wise.*"

"Yes, Marsa, ain't it the truth."

"Y'all blow that candle out here soon. We have an early day come morning." He ambled through the room.

The door swung shut.

"Putt, rut, hut, but, cut…"

I didn't flip over until I heard the thunder of a clap and saw Tommi's open hand frozen over Lucy's brown cheekbone. Mama Tommi stormed from the door.

When I jumped from the mat, sweat rolled from my body. Lucy heard the questions in my head. *Are you okay? Are we okay*?

"It don't matter, Washington. I's free now." Lucy glided toward me, held her hands out I knew to retrieve our book from me. "What part you gointa learn me now?"

I guessed I wouldn't be looking for Grandpa tonight. Why hadn't he come to find me?

Chapter 20

❧

"Sentences."

Back at the table, Lucy and I took turns reading the book. We got in the zone— together. The pages flew from letters, to words, to sentences. The sentences were super simple. *The dog ran. The man has a pen.*

The sentences then grew into little stories about people named Nat and Nell or Ben and Lucy. When Lucy first saw her name and understood that 'c' could also sound like 's', something clicked.

Lucy's entire body went limp: her eyes, her mouth, her shoulders, her back, and her hands. The book slid and crashed onto the dirt floor. Her eyes filled with twinkles and sparkles of candlelight. She was free. Lucy was free.

"Thank you, Washington." Lucy picked up the book and passed it to me. "You can have it now.

It's yours."

I gently took the book from her. Our hands touched.

Then something clicked in me. Colors became instantly brighter. The table and chairs, even the wooden walls vibrated with a pulse. The world around me looked crisper, more exact.

Reading was powerful. I was wrong. I didn't hate reading. I couldn't wait to tell Mom and tell Dad, tell Ms. Peake, tell everybody. I was wrong. I couldn't wait to tell Square.

Chapter 21

Mama Tommi entered the house, smirking as if she had been listening by the door for this exact moment. She placed two cups on the table. Herbs and dirt floated in the sweet warm milk. She moved around us, silently rearranging the sleeping mats. From the corners of her eyes she was watching us. Watching me. "It's time to go to sleep. Come morning you need to find your people. Time for restin'," she whispered as she blew out the candle.

Lucy didn't tell me the plan for the morning. I should have asked. What could be so difficult? She will show me the place where I need to go to meet Square. I would just walk out. No. What if the overseer or driver–or whatever he was–was there? Maybe there was a time of day he took his lunch break. Then she could show me and I could take the break away. I bet there's no such thing as a lunch break. My family in Henderson didn't even have 'lunch' in the future. He must leave sometime. He wasn't there when I entered. He was out searching for slaves trying to read. That's it. Somebody could give him a trick message and tell that white man that someone left the field with a book.

With that settled, I had better get some rest. But what happened when I went to sleep in the past? Square didn't tell me I could do that. Didn't want to take any chances. Grandpa George might have fallen asleep and got stuck here. I was not that tired anyway.

What were Mom and Dad doing? Today, I woke up in Houston, at home. My parents and I took a trip to the family reunion. I missed the first tournament of summer basketball. I ate some dirt on the ground. What was I thinking? I met Square. Then I met Lucy. I taught her to read. I taught her to read. That was amazing.

Earlier today I walked away from my family, ran from a book. Dirt and Square changed everything. Now I stepped in the direction of both—my family and a book.

"Rise up," Lucy said.

I wobbled on the mat from the pushing of her hands. She pointed to some clothes on the chair. I thought I had only been asleep for a minute. Now both Mama Tommi and Lucy were already awake? It was still dark outside. I was tired. The same candle sat relit on the table from the night before. I was awake early again with no basketball game to go to and no game plan to get back. I was tired. This whole no sleep practice was getting ridiculous.

Again, I copied every one of Lucy's movements. After she hid in the dark corner and changed clothes, I did, too. I carefully tied the book tightly inside layers of my white pants.

Lucy sat at the table and ate from a steaming bowl of milk, honey, and corn paste. I took sweet bites after each one of hers. No one spoke.

Mama Tommi proceeded to leave the cabin. We followed her like baby ducks. Other neighbors already sat criss cross applesauce lined in two rows in the middle of the road. Everyone was perfectly still. It was the eeriest thing I had ever seen. I was not quite sure what to expect. What were we waiting for?

A wrinkled black man walked between the people-created aisle saying random words. Two younger looking men strolled behind him burning tree branches. The smoke smelled just like the incense my family burned during the Rights of Passage drills during the reunion. The older man uttered a word to each of us as he passed.

He stopped in front of Tommi. "Grateful."

She said the word.

He paused for a moment and a big toothy smile spread across his mouth. "Free." Free was Lucy's word.

She purposefully leaned back toward me and I could hear her repeat, "Free."

Wow. My angel was free. How did he know?

The man took a step to stand in front of me. He didn't seem surprised to see me sitting in the row. The elder just took forever to give me the word.

"Dirt."

My word was "Dirt."

He waited a moment longer; he looked puzzled by the word that just escaped his lips.

I guessed the words were what you were. Because Lucy sure was free. Why would mine be dirt? Like, I was dirt? I was not sure what I felt about that. But the word "dirt" started to fill me. I breathed in that word and breathed out that word. It was a lot like how the word love sometimes felt to me. Dirt was what made this journey for me–created this time. Dirt was going to get me back to my present day family.

I was not going to live in this painting. I was not going to live in this time. I scrubbed my hands on the ground and waited.

Then he stepped to the next person in line, another boy about my age. "Truth." *Step.*

"Justice." *Step.*

"Harmony." *Step.*

"Balance." *Step.*

"Order." *Step.*

"Reciprocity." *Step.*

"Propriety…"

No sooner than the man's words were out of my hearing range, Lucy nudged me again, passing me a jar. I saw her rubbing the same cream from the jar over her arms, neck and face. It's the cinnamon cereal smell. I took some out and did the same. I rubbed it on me. The sweet scent padded the insides of my nose. The sun started to rise as the smoke from the burning branches cleared.

I figured out what we were doing. It was like our moment of silence before the game, right after Coach B said a prayer.

I thought deeply about my word *DIRT*. It was everything.

Chapter 22

We all rose and walked back up the road past the Hall toward the fields. Chatter filled the silence. Some people smiled or nodded my way, but no one talked directly to me.

This was their life? Did they ever get a chance to leave here, or did they just walk back and forth? Work back and forth?

Lucy strolled closely beside me. She made me feel safe. "Washington, who ain't a haint, do you want to jump the broom with me?"

"Excuse me?" I knew what jumping the broom meant. Was she really asking me to marry her? I was only twelve.

"Excuse me. Yes, I's asking you to jump. I said it. What's your answer? I know what my husband's gointa be like. I know what he' going to look like, too. I already know that. He looks just like you."

"I didn't know that was part of your gift, too. You can see the future?"

"Sometimes, in my dreams. Can't everybody? What's it gointa be? It's either you or Square. And I's not about to marry someone who gets caught trying to read."

My mind flashed back to all the charts in the Hall that displayed our family tree. Was Lucy the same Lucy that married my great-great-great grandfather, Square? It had to be. Ah, man. This sucked. Lucy was probably my great-great-great grandmother. I meant how many other Lucy's could there be out here?

"Lucy, you will really be free one day. You will get married, but not to me."

"Really? How you know?"

"I've got gifts, too."

She smiled shyly at my response. Washington, what is it like where you come from? Is it the same as round here, 'cept folks know how to read?"

"It's very different in my time. Everything is fast and automatic. People can make a lot of their own decisions. We aren't owned by other people. In my time, we are free." Talking about home made me feel sad. I couldn't stop feeling the sadness–homesick. "I'm ready to go back."

She nodded before she spoke. "This what we're

gointa to do. When the shadows from the trees get short, I'm going to have a fit."

I had no idea what she is talking about. "Shadows and fits?"

"Yeah, I first saw you when the shadows were gone. The shadows from the trees go from long to short, disappear, and then long again on the other side."

"Oh, okay," I said not really understanding.

"So when they start getting short, I'm a have a fit. I'll just run around any ole way hollerin', then I'm a fall to the ground." Her game face was back. "My head will be pointing straight in the direction you need to rush."

"Wow, that's cool." I was super impressed. Her plan was much better than either of mine.

"I can't run too far out, 'cause then driver will have me lashed." She abruptly stopped talking then rambled again. "You possum up to me. Pretend to check on me. Then you just go, go fast, Washington." She gave me a serious glare. "You have to be in those trees before the long shadows come–before the long shadows come round."

"Lucy Ann, will you go with me?" Things could move to the future.

"You know I can't do that." Really? Same as Imani.

The closer we got to the field, people quieted. The quiet mumbling changed to quiet whispers that changed to the near silence of only our bare feet patting the soft dirt. They walked taller with squared shoulders and chins raised. They hid smiles. So did I.

We filed in line between the dried rows of grain. The singing began, the same sad song as the day before. The white watcher guy watched. We worked. Pulling, tying, passing. My back hurt.

Time moved slowly. The shadows took forever to change sizes. It was hot. I had never been this hot in my whole life, even during blacktop pickup in the middle of August in Houston.

Right when I thought I would pass out, a giant grey cloud sailed over the scorching sun. Score. A thick breeze brushed over me. If it rains did they get to take off for the day? I bet everyone was just as happy as I. Pulling, tying, and passing to the rhythm. After a few seconds of shade, I turned to Lucy, "Don't you love clouds?"

Her face scrunched up and her eyes fill with tears.

"What is it, Lucy?" The same gloomy face Dad had when Grandpa George disappeared spread across Lucy's. Something was wrong. "What is it?"

"I can't see the shadows."

The clouds? This sucked. "What are we going to do?"

Silence.

My hushed voice exploded. "Answer me, what are we going to do?"

"We are gointa do it anyway, Washington. I's hope it's not too late." She looked at me. "You ready?"

Chapter 23

❧

Lucy darted out of line and dropped to the ground. She crawled and rolled around while she clawed at the clay. She was screeching, saying words I couldn't understand, like when Aunt Ida received the Holy-Ghost in the middle of church service.

The slaves didn't stop working; they just slowed the work line a bit. She obviously had done this before.

Mama Tommi glared through my eyes straight into my brain. She was saying even without mouthing a word, "If something happens to my girlchild, I'll kill you dead."

Lucy jumped up and ran in an eight formation. She flapped her arms like a bird about to take flight. She circled her eyes wildly then shot off running. Lucy then tripped and landed hard on her chin.

Did she do that on purpose? She didn't move. She was good. The overseer watched and waited.

Okay, I gotta go now. The sunlight began to peak through the clouds. Specks of dust filtered light shimmered around us. I searched on the ground for any traces of shadows. Shadows. Short shadows flickered. Really short. And that meant… No, no, no, no, I was almost out of time.

Like Michael Johnson sprinting a lightning 200-meter, I cut left. I ran.

I ran and I ran. Ran to Lucy. I didn't want to stay here in this time, in slavery. Time…I tried to picture my shot clock. Nothing appeared. Focus.

Shadows disappeared. No shadows anywhere. I had to be gone before they began again. So when there were no shadows, it was the middle of the day. Noon. When the shadows came back long, it would be after 12:00. What? I had less than a few minutes.

The overseer made an order for me and not Lucy. "Somebody grab that wild boy!"

I ran past Lucy. The book was why I stepped from the dirt ring, from safety. My thighs burned. I pushed harder than I had ever done before, harder than on suicides. The sun and the run made my legs feel fiery.

People chased me. They didn't run fast. They

acted like guards on the court. I ran straight. It seemed too far to where the trees began. They were too far.

I was in the crazy sci-fi stories my dad used to tell me before bedtime. Stories written by people like Octavia Butler or Stephen Barnes. The craziest events happened to people in those books. Crazy. Like this. I never imagined those things really happening to people. But now I knew. They did. Maybe one day someone would write a book about me and this. Maybe I would write it, if I ever made it out of here.

Ten more long steps stood between me and the patch of giant trees. My lungs burned. My heart raced.

Grasshoppers chimed their insane sounding referee whistles. Shadows grew over the sunlit ground. I was not going to make it.

If I couldn't make it, maybe this book could. We both didn't need to stay slaves. I reached to pull the book from inside my pants ripping the cords that held it. It wasn't there. I must have dropped it. It wasn't there.

I spun.

Grandpa George.

Tears flowed down both sides of his cheeks. His dark lips, dark gums, and very white teeth opened and closed similar to an old karate movie when the words didn't match the movements of the actor's mouth. "Reality is the state of being true."

I couldn't move my eyes away from him. He immediately snapped into screen mode, defending me, keeping me open. He found the book.

Reality was the state of being true. The truth was someone died so that I could live free and read… so that I could be, do, or have anything – the speech.

In that second, I finally thought I knew why Grandpa George stayed in slavery. He was trying to save something. Just like me.

Grandpa flashed the book in his left hand as he started. Without looking at me he long-passed it toward me. I bent my knees before the jump. Gliding in the air for more time than I thought we had left, I clapped the book tightly between both of my hands.

My soles slammed hard onto the ground. I pivoted on my left foot. Whirling around, I rocked from side to side. Where was the sun? The light was too far. Two slaves had gotten past Grandpa and double-teamed me, one on my left, and the other on my right.

"Get him boys, get that heathen darkie!"

I rocked. It was too far, but I could make it. I watched to see where sun rays shone.

The shot clock appeared in my head. The milliseconds before the last one-second dwindled away. I pulled up my elbows and rock back and forth. I was in the zone. I was the boy who couldn't miss a three. The book sat flat on my left palm. I pushed my left hand high. I reached a high arc and shot.

The book sprung out of my hand and twirled the same as a leaf flying from its tree on the first day of fall. The book swished into the light and into the trees.

Suddenly, sunlight on the ground burst apart. It created a sunny path from where I had thrown the book into the trees all the way to my feet. A game-like buzzer hummed inside my head.

Everything stilled in my vision from Grandpa George getting tackled, Mama Tommi and Lucy cheering for me, the sky, the slaves, the trees, the dirt, spun around me like a basketball on my fingertips, faster and faster. The ground around me loosened to become like quicksand.

I opened my mouth to scream for help. The sound never escaped, but I did. A glowing red dirt circle sucked at me like a giant vacuum cleaner.

'Your things can't go back in time but the things of the past can move forward. The real haints tell us that taking anything back to where you come from changes things. Changes the story, changes the reality. Taking anything- even a little speck of dirt.'

Had I done something terribly wrong?

Chapter 24

❧

The blowing and spinning stopped. My back slammed super hard into the tree, nearly knocking the wind and all of the dirt left out of me. Dirt sprayed from my mouth as I coughed.

Buffering. The world had switched. The fields of corn vanished. My people vanished. Lucy and Grandpa George–gone. I leaned next to the same tree as before–before it all. My bag and clothes draped around the base like a skirt on a Christmas tree under my bare feet.

Daylight streamed through the branches. The book slept inches from me. I palmed it. It looked like any other old book–not special. It slid from my fingertips onto my bag. I had done something terribly wrong.

People approaching shouted my name.

Muffled and muted "Washingtons" echoed

through the air–closer and closer. Mom's voice streamed louder than other calls. I also heard Lucy. Lucy. Buffering.

Scurrying to put on my shoes and clothes, I didn't know which direction to turn. I grabbed the book that I had been reading before my visit into the past, and the new one, Square's book. I hurriedly stuffed them both in my bag.

I wasn't ready to face them, or if I ever would be. What would I say? I needed more time.

A large sounding bird screeched overhead. More sounds came into focus, too. Swishing branches splashed as loud as branches crack- ing underneath my search party's soles.

What had I done? I didn't want to be here. Here where no one listened to me. Here where the most random of rules apply. I felt important in the past. What did those men do to Grandpa George? What happened to Lucy?

They had probably been punished.

What started as a slow skip turned into a quick fast tripping run. I ran away from shouts of my name. I pushed forward to the clearing and the faint wafts of cinnamon. The dirt chased me back into slavery, and it never came.

There, Mom stood in her reunion shirt and yoga pants with her back facing me, fists on her hips.

Finally, I answered. "I'm coming. I'm over here." Tears brimmed and stung my eyes. "I'm over here."

Arms open, she rushed to grab and hug me. "Do not ever scare us like that," Mom shouted. "We were about to call the fire department to start a real search for you."

"Yes ma'am," I said.

She looked at me sideways, probably because Mom insisted that I never called her ma'am. Without a breath she began barking. "You are a complete mess. Brush yourself off. We have a family photo to catch. Everybody is waiting for you. What have you been doing? This better be good."

With both hands, I pushed myself from her grasp. "Reading, like you insisted. I've been reading."

"Humph, and you didn't hear us calling for you? Really? *Really*, Washington?"

It must have clicked that she had not yet informed the other Washington searchers of my rescue.

Mom squinted at me and hollered, "Found him. I found him, y'all. We will meet you in a moment."

This was all her fault–if she had just let me play ball. What would have been in the harm in that? Now I was messed up for life. I couldn't tell what was real. *Reality is the state of being true. Reality is the state of being true.* How would I ever know what was real ever again? Was she even real? Always worried about being the best. And reading. And college. Why wasn't I allowed to just be me–be a kid?

I couldn't believe her. Could she not even look at her own only child and see the trauma I had been through? That couldn't be normal.

What freedom did I have anyway? She acted like a slave driver. I was not free. Not with them.

Is she serious? Like hey, I just spent a day enslaved with my ancestors, and almost didn't make it back. See? Why am I even here? I couldn't tell anyone what just happened. No one would believe me, not even Dad.

"What were you really doing?" Mom repeated.

"Does it even matter what I was doing?" I said.

"Excuse me? What are you saying under your breath?"

"Nothing, I didn't say anything."

While we walked in silence, I calculated real time. If our family just now gathered for the yearly reunion picture, I had only been missing, in the past, for a few hours.

Whoa!

Everyone stood shoulder to shoulder in rows behind the seated elders. The back row of family members stood on the porch of the Hall.

The people looked extra strange. Their features were misshapen and distorted. Some had eyes that were too big, or teeth that were extra-long. Their sounds, their voices, their movements were too loud. The smells of the pine and men's cologne made me queasy. I couldn't tell if I were really here. I couldn't trust my senses. Was this real?

I slithered behind the elders with the other kids as the rented cameraman snapped the photo. I wasn't smiling.

Why am I here? I tried to go inside the Hall to sort things out in my head, to be closer to Square, but after the photo Dad and Mom cornered me on one wall of the house.

"I just can't with you right now," Mom declared. "Do you plan to fix that sour face and your attitude? That was not in the least bit funny–disappearing like that. And your father was worried sick–sick to his stomach.

Hilton, have you ever seen someone so self-centered?"

"Robin, be patient. Son, I'm glad you are okay. We were a bit worried about you. Can you at least text us if you are stepping away from the group?"

And now him. He was to blame, too. He never stood up to Mom. He agreed with her craziness every single time. This sucked. Like genius, you have never even tasted the dirt. Your own father is right over there, Mr. Smart Guy.

"No," I blurted.

"No, you can't text us? If you can offer a better suggestion of communication, we are open to your thoughts."

"No, I can't fix my face." I glared my mother's direction.

"Washington," they said in unison.

My mother looked around before she lunged at me. Dad side stepped between us. "Hey, let's take a breather. We will say bye to a few folks. Why don't you wait in the car?

We can finish this conversation later." Dad leaned toward Mom tugging on her elbow to escort her away.

The sky changed colors from blue to pink. I dragged toward the only charcoal gray SUV in the dusty, raggedy parking lot.

Chapter 25

❧

Quickly, I passed the lot altogether and ventured to the path facing my trees. I wanted to go back—in the past. Apparently my people lived together, worked together, fought together. Real family. I didn't know these people here–at all. I wanted back.

Peace and safety blanketed me when I entered the wooded area. I reached down awkwardly and grabbed a handful of dirt. It sifted through my fingers. I sprinkled another sprinkling on my hand, and slowly licked it. Nothing happened.

I needed to close my eyes. Again, I tried licking the dirt faster and faster. Nothing.

Wait, should I roll dirt balls or chew it? What did I do the first time? On my hands and knees I lapped at the dirt on the ground panting like a wild dog. I had to get back. Somebody help me.

Someone was beside me. Expecting to see

Square, the edge of my lips curled, but it wasn't Square.

"Grandpa George," I said astonished.

He shook his head. "What in Sam Hill are you doing? Why are you summoning folk from the past? I need for you to cease tampering with the land. You retrieved the book. Congratulations, that was mighty fine skills you showed today. You played those boys like your Grandpa did when Dunbar Panthers took the state championship in 1963..." He laughed out loud like he had just told the best joke in the entire world. "You nearly didn't make it out in time. Did you forget something?" Grandpa George asked.

"Yes, I forgot to stay where I belong. I'm going back. I'm glad you are here to help me. So what do we need to do?" I asked him in return.

"We will do no such thing. You don't belong in the past."

"Oh, but you do? I'm doing what you did. I'm going back. I want to stay there with you—with Lucy."

"You. Don't. Belong. In. The. Past." Grandpa George clapped his hands loudly as he said each word.

"Why do you say that? I'm like you. You don't even know. While I was there, I worked. I even taught Lucy to read. I was important even without any help from you," I said to convince him.

"Look a slave's life is for no man. It is definitely not the life for my one and only grandson. I am not sure why you want to go back, but I forbid it. Over my dead body will you return today," he said.

Why was he doing this? I guessed he wasn't dead after all. "Grandpa George, I'm going back. You can't stop me."

"Young Washington, I've always lived between two worlds. Living was fighting. When I grew up, we lived legalized slavery, Jim Crowe. We had to fight. We had to fight for balance. We had to fight to attend schools. We had to fight for everything, except to stay Black. They let us have that. We started fightin' each other. Then they ordered me off to fight in the Vietnam War. Two worlds, Washington." He paused. "Your dad's generation was the first almost free African Americans in the Americans, and you the second. Don't you understand? I fought for you, for my boy, for you, Washington because you matter." The bones in his jaws rippled beneath his skin. "Your life matters. You are not meant to exist between two worlds of present and past."

"Why are you living in the past after all of that fighting?" I questioned.

"It's my calling. I was called to stay in the past. You've heard of haints or ghosts? Sometimes spirits travel from a past world and stick around to help people and relay messages to the present world. Well, I'm the reverse of that. I'm a present ghost that returns to help the people of the past. I have messages for them to make sure that our lineage carries on and thrives. There is no way to escape your calling. This is what I was called to do –purpose. I had to do it."

"Maybe I'm called to stay in the past like you were. Why is that so impossible to believe?"

"Stubborn like Hilton, I see. Did you feel you had to get Square's book?"

"Yes, sir."

"Why?" Grandpa George leaned toward me.

"At first I didn't want anyone else to get hurt because of it. I figured out a few things with that book. I figured out a different thing about myself. I don't know how to really explain it. It just happened. It just happened," I said.

"That book was mighty important to me. It is very important. That was only a piece of my job. Your job is revealed in the scene you enter. One of my jobs is to protect the land. I help others with the jobs they are sent to complete. I can't really get hurt in the past. The dirt protects me. Another task is to make sure that knuckle heads like you don't stay in the past and meddle it all up. I have to make sure that you go home. Take your tools.

Take the book and go home."

Could I just ignore what he was saying? What would happen if I just starting making dirt balls?

"You can do it, Young Square. You can do it if you saved the book you can do any- thing. Now, I do think you were meant to come get that book. When my son didn't come back to slavery, I thought that it was finished. I thought that it was done. I didn't think that mine would have to come back here when I protected the land. But I felt you, I followed you on the other side. I'm always there," he said sadly. "What did you see when you were staying with Lucy? Did you see that they didn't have choice? Did you see that they did not have freedoms? Washington, they couldn't even read the book."

His speeches could probably go on forever –much longer than any of Mom's. I really didn't know if I could live like Lucy. He had already promised that I wasn't going back today. And he was right about everything. I was being really ridiculous.

"You are worth more than that," he continued. "You can do, be, or have anything that you want. But you can't do that living in the past. You can't do that going back there. They are in the past. They are gone. They are no longer. They fought the fight for you to be free. Those people in that time are no longer real. They don't matter, now. Your life matters. Now go on back go back and do something wonderful."

"Okay, okay, okay," I said. "What about the book?"

"Well I guess you are the guardian of the book. Yep, that makes you the guardian of the written word for our family. That's what it looks like to me. The fierceness you displayed, the passion you showed. You were willing to save the book above yourself. I am proud of you. I'm so pleased at what you have become. If you were called to get the book and take it back, you are the guardian of the book. Do something wonderful with the book. I love you, Young Square. I love you."

I lit up inside when he called me Young Square for the second time. It sounded regal, and reminded me of some missing scene from the Lion King between Mufasa and Cimba with Zazu circling overhead. Grandpa George was right. Just like I knew I had to get the book. I knew he was right, and that I had been wrong–very wrong.

I hugged him and cried. He disintegrated and dissolved as I if I were squeezing a life size sand castle. He was right.

By the time my parents returned to the car, I was pretend-sleep in the back seat. This time Dad sat in the driver's seat.

Chapter 26

❧

We travelled in complete silence. Even though I was tired, I couldn't sleep. Why would a book be my calling? I guessed I didn't really hate reading, but a book as my calling? Calling me to read? That seemed basic. What did Grandpa George mean–do something wonderful with the book?

I wanted to understand what to do with the book. What can you do with a book? It's a book. A basic book—I could read it. I guess it's an antique. I could sell it. I really didn't know.

What could I do with the book? I taught Lucy how to read. Maybe I should teach. I just didn't think that was it. Maybe, I would become a coach like my grandpa. Coaches had to teach, too. I didn't know. I had heard about people getting their calling from the Bible. And that's a book. Maybe I was supposed to start preaching about reading.

I was dizzy. The world switched. Some-how I knew in my dream that I was dreaming. The blowing and spinning quit. Chicks chirped. No. Rubber-soled sneakers scraped against a hard wood court. The whistle squealed. Go.

"Mind the clock, Washing, get your head in the game," Coach B yelled while he jumped up and down.

The clock raced to the game's second ending. My Monarch teammate chest-passed me the assist. I pulled up my elbows up and rocked back and forth. I was in the three zone. The ball sat flat on my left palm. I pushed off with my hand high. I reached a high arc and shot. My arm lingered in the air with all my fingers pointing downward. I couldn't miss; I was the boy who never missed a three. We all focused on the net-SWISH. We won the game by a single point in overtime.

I bounded toward Coach. He lifted me over his shoulder while my teammates ran from their posts around the gym to surround us.

From on top of Coach's shoulders, I spotted Ms. Peake and Mom. Mom grinned like that cat from Alice in Wonderland in the stands. She looked even happier than I felt. Dad looked happy, too. He and Grandpa George stood next to her giving each other high-five.

Coach tossed me down as quickly as he'd lifted

me. His voice matched his body. Both demanded complete attention. "Good run, guys, Monarchs on three. One… two… three…"

With a Huey P. Black power fist, we all cheered "Monarchs!"

Our black and orange traveling uniforms were the best of all the teams. The slick black pants buttoned down the sides with tiny basketball snap buttons. In fancy cursive orange letters our black silky jackets had 'Monarchs' sewn on the left side. And on mine, Wash the Three #13, of course, was written with the same lettering on the right.

We were lined up in number order on the floor, one behind the next. Someone sang the National Anthem, then some commissioner person thanked all the teams for participating. I read the back of #7's jacket and shined with pride. The backs to all of our uniforms had the same words: Sponsored by Square Thompson's African American Reading Gallery.

Then I flew into Mom's gallery through one of the windows, but this gallery was the coolest place. Literature fanatics stood around just to see the items Mom displayed. There was stuff all about books for and by famous Black Americans. Famous Black writers read from their latest works on the different levels of the warehouse—Jacquelin Thomas, Christopher Paul Curtis, Sharon Flake, and Walter Dean Myers.

I landed now wearing white cottony gloves. I carefully pulled out the book that set in its own glass case in the entrance. The slippery cover seemed to melt underneath the cotton gloves. Some of the gray letters from the title could still be read. The book's brownness matched the couches in our living room. Turning each yellowed page crackled like an empty candy wrapper. The pages didn't really say much–just the alphabet, a bunch of little words, and a few poems. One page felt more flimsy than the others. There were only two items on it–a picture of a square with the word square written underneath.

Flashing lights and beeping noises awoke me. We were in our driveway at home. I remembered it all. Did I just see the future in my dream? Thank you, Lucy.

"Wait, please don't get out of the car yet. I need to say something," I said.

Mom sighed and started to say something.

"Please listen. Can you please just listen to me?" My voice showed that I meant business.

They remained silent.

"Okay, Mom, Dad, look, I haven't been the smartest lately. I think going to the land really changed me this time." My breathing slowed to a steady pace. "I feel differently about a lot of things.

I feel differently about reading. I feel differently about my family. I need for you guys to know that."

Dad spoke. "Go on, son."

"I'm sorry. I'm so sorry. I've been selfish. I shouldn't have left like I did, but I needed to get away!" I paused trying to put together which parts I wanted to share. "And when I was gone I found a book. I brought it back and I have it with me. It's a really old book and I think you guys should, or we should do something with it. Maybe we could change the art gallery to a gallery of books. A history of African-Americans reading and writing — is there even anything like that? This new place could show the journey of reading and writing by Black people for Black people about Black people." My voice steadied. "I don't think it's enough to tell people that some other older people died, so that we could be free and read. I think we need to show them and I think that we can use this book and other books and I just think it will work out, Mom. I think that the gallery should change directions and I'm going to change directions, too. I'm going to try to take read- ing and school more seriously. And I'm not going to take basketball as serious." I finally took another breath again.

"Let me see this book you're talking about. Where exactly did you find it?" Dad twisted fully around in his seat and observed me.

My heart raced and I felt that my story and my speech had not been entirely believable. I passed the book forward to him.

The interior lights of the car beamed all around us while a few bugs whizzed around us. Seconds turned into minutes and we still sat in silence.

"Well, I'll be. I've always thought it was fabricated. It's a real…the book is real, Robin. It's not some family urban tale. The book is real. You see, there is a story an urban legend of sorts in my family that I never told you two about. I didn't know how true it was." His voice trailed into a whisper.

Dad's face was relaxed. I didn't know that I had ever seen his relaxed face in real life. I'd seen it in photos–photos before Grandpa George left. He sounded like a little kid. My Dad had never sounded like a little kid.

"Where did you say you found this again? He didn't ask the question like he really want- ed me to answer. He asked it as if he wanted me to know that he knew.

Both of them focused completely on me, then we talked.

We talked in the car for a while about the book, the family and tons of other things. Wow, they were actually listening to me. This didn't suck at all.

Mom's eyes glistened. "I think a literature gallery is such a fantastic idea. Let's go inside.

I want to hear more."

I walked in from the car and pocketed the shiny family reunion reminder postcard that still sat on the credenza in the entry. I couldn't wait for my classes to start with Ms. Peake. I looked up and rolled my head back. The mural on our front entry ceiling with colors of root beer floats pulled at my vision.

Ebhochimbo.

Love Note from the Author

Thank you for exploring *Dirt.*

One of the larger problems with the manuscript, *Dirt,* is its size. It is rather small to be published as a traditional novel. I appreciate Brown Girls Books for taking the risk to publish a very small novel. The initial goal in the writing of *Dirt* was to create a hybrid between a chapter book and a middle grade novel that focused on a good story for a wide range of middle grade audiences – a hi-lo reader with extreme depth. And it had to be about the importance of literacy and reading.

Literacy is the seventh sense. We read our world through our senses. Much like sight, sound, smell, taste, touch and intuition, we inventory our surroundings through words. Words tell us when to stop, and when to go.

It has been noted that when one of our sensory organs fail, the other organs work harder to compensate for the deficit. Blind people's hearing is often more acute. During my life and my life as an at-risk educator, I have come across many non-literate people. Statistics report that most adult Americans read English at least at an eighth grade level, a qualifier for literacy. I have met many who do not read at this level. Their reasons are varied: some are new to this country, have a learning difference or experience trauma during their reading foundational years.

Whatever their road to illiteracy entailed, one thing is consistent - their coping skills are phenomenal. They are amazing. What they lack in reading, they make up in wit, attitude, phonographic memories, photographic memories, artistic ability...the list goes on.

I have a really hard time believing that anyone HATES READING like Washington often laments.

My very own late Aunt Marie struggled to read. I did not know this until near the end of her life. She created recipes and baked like nobody's business. Laughter, music, movies and sweets filled her tiny home.

Our holiday past time was coloring in giant -sized coloring books. She spent hours having me read books into tape recorders to her when I was young. I still have a tape somewhere where she interviewed me about the books I had authored as if I were on a late night talk show. I was eight years old at the time.

Her memory was astute and her attitude was fierce. She could style anyone from head- to-toe. She was a home beautician by trade. She even pierced my ears at my grandmother's house when broomstick fillers were needed. I never viewed our interactions as a compensation for her ability to code written words. It probably was.

This leads me to imagine that a part of the reason that Black American Slaves were a mystical and magical subset of our historic population is the fact that they were denied a traditional route to literacy, or access to education. An entire national community evolved to interpret and decode the world through a myriad of devices that didn't include the written world. All of their senses were obviously heightened. Slaves had to rely on developing interpretive tools–dreams, nature, intuition, storytelling, empathic devices and their memory among others to make sense of the world, communicate with one another and even survive.

Our family histories are so telling. On my mother's side of the family many slave survivors could read and write according to their archived census reports.

As for the Thompsons, I'm not quite sure. My great-great grandmother, the real wife of the real Square was named Lucy. I'm not sure if she could read or write. I haven't researched her real story.

Lucy in Dirt represents this mystical magical thought. So, to honor my Aunt Marie, Lucy appears. We love Lucy. I'm hoping to find out more about her (the family version or the fictional version). I'm hoping that we can remove the stigma of shame and love our reading struggling population like we love Lucy, like I loved Marie into learning to read, in to loving to read.

If you are struggling with words or know someone that is, please contact me: @teffanie on twitter or reference my blog: http://freecottonclub.blogspot.com/.

You are not forgotten and your journey is remembered.

Love…

Questions and Topics for Discussion

1. What elements of literature or literary devices can you identify within the text?

2. Washington's parents punished him for his low reading grade by canceling his involvement in team sports. Should parents or schools totally eliminate extracurricular participation for low or failing grades or should there be more of a three strikes you're out rule?

3. Do you think Washington's parents made a good choice by making him go to the family reunion instead of playing in the basketball tournament? Why or why not? What about his commitment to his team?

4. Have you ever felt unjustly punished? By whom? For what?

5. What could interfere with giving adequate importance to books today? What are people doing besides reading? How can we share the love of the written word without a life changing time travel experience?

6. Prior to meeting him, what is the significance of Square being drawn to the mural on the ceiling and to Square's photo?

7. With the competition so fierce in professional sports and entertainment why do so many young people aspire for professions in these particular fields?

8. Why do you believe that dirt doubles as the time and space travel mechanism? What could be some of the symbolic references for dirt in the novel Dirt?

9. Dirt is universally abundant. Would you ever eat dirt? Are there communities or cultures that have dirt as a part of their diet? What's the history of this practice?

10. Besides missing the basketball tournament, why do you believe Washington was resistant to going to the family reunion?

11. What purpose do family reunions serve? Why are they important to continue for both the older and younger generations? Have you ever attended a family reunion? How was it?

12. What does reading represent to both the slave and to the slave owner? Would you be willing to give your life for learning to read, or for getting an education? Could you imagine denying a group of people access to learning? They are many groups globally that have limited access to education. Who are they?

13. In your opinion was Square's loss of eyesight worth the risk of trying to learn to read? Have you ever risked something of great importance, in order to have something of equal or greater importance?

14. How might Washington's present family situation be different if his family's commitment to education had not been as strong?

15. We were presented a brief historically fictionalized sketch of community life during slavery. How are our communities the same? How are they different?

16. An underlying presentation in Dirt is the acknowledgment of recent African American firsts. Many of the names in the book are actual famous people. Can you find them? What is their known societal contribution?

17. What is reality?

Extension Activities

1. Interpret the haiku that begins the book.

2. Create a family tree.

3. Research your own family's heroes.

4. Plan a family reunion for real or for fun.

5. Submit self-created art that complements the text to be featured on our social media platforms to: http://picturelessbooks.blogspot.com

6. Write a letter to an ancestor that helped to give you your current day liberties.

7. Talk to your oldest living relatives, and ask them their stories.

8. Share this book with non-reading loving people.

9. Read more books.

Discussion Question Contributors

Danielle McGill Hinesly
Margaret Hover
Roberta Shook
Rose Thompson

CPSIA information can be obtained
at www.ICGtesting.com
Printed in the USA
FSHW021313250220
67520FS